Soul on Nice

Norm Spitzig

A Clive and Esther Reprise Novel of Global Travel, Whimsical Humor, Private Club Life, Political Satire, and International Intrigue

First published by Dog Ear Publishing
4010 W. 86th Street, Ste H
Indianapolis, IN 46268
www.dogearpublishing.net

dog ear PUBLISHING

ISBN: 978-1-45752-170-6

This is a work of fiction. The author made up this stuff.

This book—oh, happy days!—is printed on acid-free paper.

Printed in the United States of America

Praise for Norm Spitzig's Books

"Clive's wonderful books have given me lots of chuckles and some humongous belly laughs. I have bought copies for our general manager, our club officers, and our entire Board of Directors."

—Norm Matthew

"Clive (Norm) accurately captures the fanciful foibles—and, at times, the 'wonderful lunacy'—in the private club environment. His many characters, who seem to be right out of central casting, can be found frolicking about in utter abandon throughout the book. *I know* these people—*you know* these people! Every page is a hoot and laugh-out-loud moment. **Private Clubs in America and around the World** is a *great* read!"

—Peter Kite

"I believe that Clive Endive Ogive IV (Norm Spitzig) is, without question, the most insightful and accomplished writer *ever* regarding the wonderful world of private clubs. **Private Clubs in American and around the World** is an absolute must-read for those who have ever been associated with private clubs and, more importantly, *anyone* who has a sense of humor. I am a loyal and devoted fan."

—Terry Gilmer

“**Murder and Mayhem at Old Bunbury** is a gleeful parody of the stereotypical private club, with its selective membership, distaste for the hoi polloi, and a zany cast of über-rich oddballs with some of the silliest names you’re likely to encounter outside of a P.G. Wodehouse novel. The club, Old Bunbury, is nothing short of a riotous temple to old-school capitalism and Clive Endive Ogive IV its devoted high priest.”

—Lavanya Karthik

“I just finished **How Now, Norm’s Tao** this morning. What a fantastic read! Norm’s stories would make for a great movie. A reality show centered around a private club would be a huge hit. Pay attention, Hollywood!”

—Bill Horton

“Using captivating personal stories, linguistic prowess, and acerbic wit, Norm shares twelve life lessons learned through his professional and life experience. Though most of the stories have their foundation in the private club world, their value and impact transcend private clubs. From lessons on dealing with difficult people, to the value of giving more and expecting less, to overcoming challenging situations, every person in every walk of life will find a way to appreciate and apply the wisdom found in **How Now, Norm’s Tao**.”

—Jason Rutherford

"Set against the backdrop of a lifelong career in the private club industry, **How Now, Norm's Tao** delves into the accomplished life of entrepreneur Norm Spitzig and surfaces with a baker's dozen of timeless universal lessons. This witty memoir illuminates the secrets of a life well lived and expounds upon the core principles that have kept a twinkle in Norm's eye and a spring in his step. His sincere, captivating stories are a recipe for inspiration, practical thinking, and, most importantly, laughter."

—Bill Johnson

"Clive Endive Ogive IV is the Bodhisattva for the world of private clubs."

—Arch Stokes

"Being a good Catholic boy, I cannot tell a lie. I just finished **How Now, Norm's Tao**. I thoroughly enjoyed the read and can relate to many of the experiences. As a matter of fact, next Tuesday I am having breakfast with the new president of a wonderful private club and will strongly recommend that he follow 'one man's path to a more enjoyable personal life and rewarding professional career.'"

—Jim Butler

"If you like the biting sarcasm of Nelson DeMille's John Corey, the charismatic intellect of John LeCarré's George Smiley, and the irreverent wit of Michael Connelly's Harry Bosch, you will love the world of Norm Spitzig's Clive and Esther."

—Anne Richardson

"Norm Spitzig is that rare linguistic artist who fully understands and appreciates the evocative power and unfettered playfulness of properly chosen words."

—Dan Wilson

To Cody, Katie, Colleen, Claire, Josie, Charlotte, Lucy, and Paisley—my special bevy of beauties.

Also by Norm Spitzig

How Now, Norm's Tao

Murder and Mayhem at Old Bunbury (under the nom de plume Clive Endive Ogive IV)

Private Clubs in America and around the World (under the nom de plume Clive Endive Ogive IV)

Perspectives on Club Management

"I have nothing to declare but my genius."

—Oscar Wilde

"A friend of the devil is a friend of mine."

—Jerry Garcia

"Lead your way
Sing your song
Moving every day
Going further on."

—Bronze Radio Return

"In a world of universal deceit,
telling the truth is a revolutionary act."

—George Orwell

Table of Contents

Part II: The United States

Socrates Speaks

Well, it's about time! Here I am, Socrates, indubitably the eldest, wisest, best looking, and most humble member of the Big Three of ancient Greek philosophy, but I was still chosen *last* to write the foreword to one of Norm Spitzig's wonderful books. Ain't *that* a kick in the old tunic! Maybe it's because, unlike Plato and Aristotle, I didn't take the time to write down any of my ideas; the spoken word—remember, we lived in the dark ages before texting and movable type—was always good enough for me. Whatever. Anyway, I guess I was right when I first said all those centuries ago that "good things do indeed come those who wait"—yes, that was a Socrates original. My star pupil, Plato, will confirm it. As you can probably deduce, I do have quite a bit of time on my hands. Let me tell you mortals one thing: This eternity gig isn't all it's cracked up to be.

Norm, thanks again for asking me to help out. I know that you were a philosophy and mathematics double major at Boston College and, as such, are an ethical, fair, and logical guy. Yes, it took you a while to complete your "introduction trilogy duties," but I never doubted that you would eventually come through. Okay, maybe a bit.

So here goes. Norm's latest book chronicles the continuing adventures of the Old Bunbury Golf Links & Reading Club's waitress-extraordinaire, Esther, the highly eccentric but undeniably lovable protagonist of his previous epic works. This time, Norm's scintillating tale is truly global in scope, with Esther opening the novel zooming her merry old way to New Zealand. I certainly won't provide you with any spoilers for this titanic clash between good and evil other than to say that the book is part playful and evocative travelogue, part staunch conservative manifesto, part clever and poignant mystery, part whimsical exposé of the madcap world of private clubs, and *all* treasure trove of quirky good cheer. While anyone with a modicum of self-respect, a reasonable work ethic, and a decent sense of humor—in other words, a conservative—will surely love Norm's latest story, readers who also understand and appreciate the fascinating world of private clubs will be doubly pleased. There's no doubt that *Soul on Nice* is slated to become another Norm Spitzig classic.

You may have heard this before, but I was a proud Founding Member of one of the finest private clubs ever to exist—the Old Philosophers & Young Boys Club in downtown Athens. We were a pretty exclusive club, if I do say so myself. We had spacious, well-staffed hot baths, tastefully decorated reading rooms that contained the finest Alexandrian scrolls money could buy, and a colonnade-style bar stocked with exotic adult libations from all around the civilized world. I think this was why the club had such a long waiting list. Heck, it was only because of my strong endorsement that Plato and Aristotle were even considered for admission. As I recall, the Membership Committee thought Plato was too damned cerebral and Aristotle too much of a condescending prig. Sure, those guys had encyclopedic minds and could sometimes be geeks, but they also knew how to cut loose when the occasion called for it.

Norm, lest any of you forget, is a 112th-generation direct descendent of Plato and his not-so-lovely wife Xanthippe. Come to think of it, that Xanthippe was a real piece of work, always complaining how we wouldn't let her into the club. I kept telling her that, back in those admittedly dark days, private clubs didn't admit *any* women, but she just never got it. But no worries. For what it's worth, I, for one, actually *like* how private clubs have become more open-minded in the modern world. Heck, I know one club in Florida where the only current criteria for admission are that your initiation fee check clears and you are breathing—and the Membership Committee is pretty flexible on the latter. A lot of traditionalists in the eternity crowd, like living Senior Members the world over, are still grappling with all these newfangled ideas. *So what else is new!*

The bottom line is this: It is my sincere desire that you read and enjoy this latest offering from Norm Spitzig. If you like it, spread the word. If not, well, may it be your destiny to join me here in eternity *real* soon.

Shortly after the untimely demise of Socrates, the Old Philosophers & Young Boys Club Board of Directors wisely removed hemlock from the libations menu.

Part I

New Zealand

Chapter 1

The Return to New Zealand

The thought that this was her fifth visit to New Zealand randomly flitted through her semiconscious mind. No, sixth, Esther immediately corrected herself as, with Herculean effort, she forced herself back to a state of full alertness. Uncharacteristically, she'd had a momentary mental lapse about the two wonderful weeks she had spent meandering about The Catlins in the fall of 2006. How could she have ever forgotten *that* glorious trip, if even for only a second—perhaps her most cherished visit of all to the land of Kiwis and Maoris?

Esther absolutely *loved* New Zealand. It was her undeniably favorite country (other than the good old US of A, of course—the land of her birth and lifelong residence) in the entire world—and The Catlins was one of Esther's favorite parts of the country. She relished the fact that the area, not much more than a hundred square miles between Kaka Point and Fortrose on the South Island, was little known and sparsely populated, even by New Zealand standards. She feasted on the exquisite beauty of the rugged coastlines, the stunningly beautiful waterfalls, the lush temperate forests, and the hidden, crystal clear lakes. She savored the peaceful solitude that permeated every single bone of her spindly yet surprisingly strong body as she happily roamed the resplendent countryside from one spectacular place to the next. Ah, Nugget Point, Purakaunui Falls, Cathedral Caves, Curio Bay, and the exceptionally mouth-watering cuisine at the quaint Niagara Falls Cafe (one of Esther's very favorite restaurants in the entire world). Life in this world just doesn't get any better. Esther couldn't restrain her growing smile as the splendid details of the trip came flooding back.

Esther had been dozing in seat 3B aboard Air New Zealand flight NZ0001 bound for Auckland out of Los Angeles. She had treated herself to an upgrade to Business Premier on the twelve-and-a-half-hour flight and wanted to enjoy every minute of it. The Boeing "Triple Seven" was one helluva plane, she thought, especially the way Air New Zealand had royally outfitted and staffed its impressive fleet for these long-haul flights.

"May I bring you another glass of Chardonnay?" asked the attentive and attractive flight attendant. Her name was Naomi, and she and Esther had been chatting off and on since the plane had left the ground. Esther mused, not for the first time, that Naomi's facial features confirmed that she had some Maori blood in her.

"Yes, I do believe I'll have one more," replied Esther. Yes, she was going to savor every single moment on this luxurious journey across the vast Pacific.

"I love the fact that we left Los Angeles on a Wednesday night and will arrive in Auckland on Friday morning," Esther continued, the enthusiasm unmistakable in her high-pitched voice. "It's just plain weird, even though I know that it is also perfectly logical. Does that make any sense, Naomi?"

"Yes, Esther, it does. I must admit that your astute observation fascinates me as well—and I make this long trip twice a month. Ah, the wonders of modern air travel and rapid time-zone changes." As she handed Esther her glass of Jackson Estate Shelter Belt 2011 Chardonnay, Naomi added, "Remember, I'm here if you need anything. Anything at all. Just ask. On Air New Zealand, we're always ready to cater to our Business Premier customers' every whim. And besides that, you're a very nice person, Esther."

"Thank you so much," Esther replied with characteristic graciousness, taking a small sip of her wine. Three glasses of Chardonnay was pushing her limit, but now and again, special occasions won out over temperance. Yes, this was going to be a *great* trip.

Not that Esther's mind was slipping, mind you. To the contrary, her memory was as sharp as ever, despite her advancing age. As anyone who knew Esther would attest, the topic of her age was strictly taboo. Bringing it up was one of the very few things that might very well send Esther into a bout of apoplectic rage. That, and a conversation with a pretentious liberal. (Now *there's* a tautology if there ever was one!) Esther could still proudly recite the names of every single member (both alphabetically and by date of seniority—take your pick) of the Old Bunbury Golf Links & Reading Club, the very prestigious and ultra-exclusive private club that had employed her as a waitress for far longer than she, or anyone one else, dared openly admit. She knew, at any given time, who was boinking whom as well as when, where, and why. She knew the exact net worth, dark family secrets, and furtive desires of everyone associated with the club for the past half century. Esther could rattle off the names of the Old Bunbury presidents as quickly as she could the presidents of the United States. (She always stopped at George Walker Bush. For Esther, as for the vast majority of rational, freedom-loving Americans everywhere, Barack Hussein Obama just didn't count.) In short, Esther knew far, far more than was necessary to guarantee her lifetime employment at the club (should someone ever be so foolish as to actually try to get rid of her). Esther was more of a fixture at Old Bunbury than the seedy mauve and tan tartan divan that, for the past five decades, had unceremoniously graced the purposely nondescript entrance foyer to the club.

This time, in fact, Esther was going to New Zealand compliments of the Board of Directors of Old Bunbury. The club's long-time president, Clive Endive Ogive IV—her absolutely all-time favorite Old Bunbury member, and that was saying something—had told her that this was her reward for solving the hideous murder of Alfie Johnson. (Esther, as you might have expected, had already known about the Board of Directors' largess in this regard long before President Clive actually delivered the good news.) Alfie had been brutally bludgeoned to death with a five iron and hastily dumped right behind the club's fourteenth green—the club's signature hole, no less. It was a gruesome affair—and also an especially trying and embarrassing time in the long and storied history of Old Bunbury. To the relief of all concerned, Esther's encyclopedic knowledge of all things Old Bunbury, her dogged pursuit of the truth, and her previously unknown but considerable detective skills had brought the entire sordid episode to a quick and successful conclusion.

As a result of her sleuthing success, Esther had gained a fair amount of notoriety, with both the members of the club and the residents of the local community. Even those members who didn't much like Esther—every private club surely has its share of miscreants and ne'er-do-wells—began to show her begrudging respect. Not that Esther cared a possum's patootie about any of it. At her core, Esther was an extremely private and fiercely independent person who kept mostly to herself. Although she truly enjoyed working at Old Bunbury and always had tried her very best (in her own unorthodox, quirky sort of way) to make the members happy—at least those she personally liked, when her travel schedule allowed—she also was one of those rare people who was truly comfortable being alone. Esther embraced solitude more than a Democrat embraces big government.

Over time, Esther's newfound fame began to spread beyond the confines of the ivied walls of the club and the nearby residents' gossip. When Esther's sleuthing success story became known to Old Bunbury's sister club—the Kaikoura Whaling & Sailing Club—in faraway New Zealand, it was only a matter of time before the leadership at both clubs agreed that something should be done about it. Esther's visit to New Zealand was deemed the perfect opportunity for the Kaikoura membership to meet and appropriately honor the best waitress-detective in the wonderful world of private clubs, and plans for a personalized afternoon tour of the club (by no less than the Kaikoura Whaling & Sailing Club president himself) followed by a gala appreciation dinner were quickly put into place. Esther had at first balked but, in the end, reluctantly agreed, primarily as a favor to President Ogive. Besides, she thought, it might actually be fun to visit one of the very few private clubs in the entire world that comfortably and unpretentiously dwelt in the same rarified and lofty air as Old Bunbury.

Esther took another sip of her Shelter Belt, one of the Marlborough wine region's most highly regarded, and began to browse the extensive movie selection available to Business Premier flyers as the Boeing jumbo jet pushed steadily on through the starry darkness.

Esther never tires of the peaceful solitude and stark beauty of the craggy, windswept walk to the remote Nugget Point Lighthouse.

Chapter 2

On New Zealand Soil

New Zealand flight NZ0001 touched down at Auckland International thirty-two minutes ahead of schedule, thanks in no small part to the eighty-plus mile-per-hour tailwinds that had helped push the plane for most of the flight. As the jet slowly taxied to the international terminal, Esther extended her good-byes to Naomi.

"Thank you again for making my flight so memorable, Naomi. You're the best."

"Thank *you*, Esther," replied Naomi fondly. "It's the exceptionally kind passengers like yourself who make my job all the more enjoyable and rewarding. I hope you have a wonderful visit to my beautiful homeland, Aotearoa."

Aotearoa. Most commonly translated as "the land of the long white cloud." Esther had been long aware that Aotearoa was the native Maori name for New Zealand and that the true origins and exact meaning of the word had long been shrouded in historical fiction or mythological storytelling. Though certainly no expert on Maori culture, Esther knew substantially more than the typical New Zealander—and *far* more than any American she had ever met—about the long, and often troubled, history of the Maori tribe in New Zealand. She was, in point of fact, fascinated by all things Maori. It was just one of the many reasons why Esther so loved New Zealand.

On this particular trip, Esther was planning to start in Christchurch, re-explore the metropolitan area for two or three days—she hadn't been there since the devastating earthquake in February 2011—and then head north on Route 1 to Kaikoura, where she would politely tour the Whaling & Sailing Club, dutifully attend Saturday's celebratory dinner in her honor, and then quickly head out on her own. Though Esther had a general sense of what she wanted to see and accomplish on this particular New Zealand vacation—she planned to concentrate on the South Island—she was never much one to over-think things. After Kaikoura, Esther would play it by ear. It was the manner in which she traveled best.

Esther made her way through customs without incident and decided, rather than take the shuttle, to walk to the domestic terminal. Her luggage had been checked directly through to Christchurch, and the next flight she was on—NZ504—didn't leave for close to two and a half hours. Twelve minutes at a brisk pace would go a long way towards loosening up Esther's stiffened legs. She was in decent physical shape, especially for someone her age, but thirteen cramped and claustrophobic hours on an airplane, no matter how luxuriously outfitted, are sufficient to substantially fatigue even the best-trained Olympic athlete.

Not much of a shopper, Esther decided to spend her time waiting to board Air New Zealand flight NZ504 by catching up on e-mails and responding to any text messages she might have received. (Esther's current smart phone of choice was the sleek and powerful new Apple iPhone 5. Unalterably set in her ways on most things, Esther nevertheless did her best to keep up with technology and didn't exhibit much patience or respect for people who were unwilling or unable to do so.) After dealing with those few e-mails that required replies and deleting the far larger number that did not, Esther responded to the gracious text she had received from Old Bunbury Club President Clive Ogive. He had sent her his personal best wishes for a safe and enjoyable sixth visit to New Zealand, to which Esther meticulously keyed back, "Thanks, boss. I will. I've landed safely in Auckland and will soon be on my way to Christchurch. After that, it's on to the festivities at the Kaikoura Whaling & Sailing Club. I'll let you know how the evening goes. Thanks again for all your help in setting up this dinner. As I've already told you, it certainly wasn't necessary, but rest assured that I will do my very best to represent Old Bunbury with class and integrity. Please give my regards to everyone back at the club."

The one-and-a-half–hour flight to Christchurch was uneventful—always a good thing when one is traveling by air—and, after landing and recovering her luggage, Esther found herself at the Hertz counter in the drab, in-need-of-major-remodeling lower level of Christchurch International.

"Good morning, young man. I'd like to pick up my car. Here are the details of my reservation," Esther said cheerily, handing him her readied paperwork. His name was Stuart X. Thurpleman; either that, or he had lost his own nametag and surreptitiously "borrowed" one from a fellow coworker.

"Certainly, ma'am," Stuart returned in the distinct and, to Esther's ears, always fascinating and alluring New Zealand accent as he simultaneously discarded yesterday's sports section of the *Christchurch Star* and donned his best customer smile. (Esther had traveled the United States, England, Ireland, Scotland, Australia, South Africa, Canada, and New Zealand long and extensively enough to recognize a good amount of the subtle differences between the English spoken in each country. New Zealanders, for example, are unique in pronouncing the *e* in words like "beg" and "Greg" like the vowel sound found in the words "leak" and "Greek." Also, when a Kiwi says, "The cat with a hat sat on the mat"—assuming, of course, that he or she would have reason to make such a statement—it sounds far closer to "The ket with a het set on the met." To Esther's way of thinking, though, the undeniably best way for verifying whether one is listening to a native Australian or native New Zealander lies in how he or she pronounces the letter *i*. If the person claims to enjoy "feesh and cheeps," he or she is probably an Australian. If, on the other hand, he or she prefers "fush and chups," you are most likely dealing with a New Zealander.)

Reading her name and confirming that the reservation was legitimate, Stuart began dutifully preparing the extensive reams of paperwork that were apparently required to successfully rent a car in New Zealand. *Why in the world do we need all this paperwork?* Esther wondered. Every time she visited the land of the storied All Blacks—the legendary and near-invincible New Zealand men's national rugby union team—Esther became quickly irked by the fact that, as courteous and efficient as Hertz was with its customers back in the United States—she was a long-time Five Star Gold member and firmly believed that, all things considered, the company was the very best in the rental-car business—New Zealand franchisees seemed to prepare very little paperwork, if any, in advance. *Maybe there are a lot of rental car no-shows in Kiwi land.* For whatever reason, her cherished Five Star Gold status in the United States seemed to carry no weight whatsoever with Hertz franchisees in this part of the world. Perhaps the Hertz employees in New Zealand had been "trained" by the United States federal government, the acknowledged world leaders in senseless paperwork and bloated, inefficient bureaucracy. Before she was finished, Esther calculated that she had dutifully placed her initials on seven assorted forms in thirteen spots as well as signed her full name nine times. *Any more of this, and I'll get writer's cramp. I'm renting a car, not buying a house.* Esther, however, remained professional and polite—as did Stuart, who was clearly proceeding as quickly as he could—throughout what she deemed a tedious and unnecessary process, and an agonizingly slow and painfully irritating twenty-seven minutes later, she was seated in a low-mileage 2013 red Toyota Camry LE, still breathing heavily but eager to hit the road. *Get over it,* she told herself yet again. *Take deep breaths. Slowly, in and out. This is a* very *minor glitch. If the only thing that I can find "bad" about New Zealand is the fact that it takes too long to pick up a rental car, then life is good here.* Very *good.* Three minutes later, Esther was once again her calm and collected self and she turned the key in the ignition.

The quaint little Niagara Falls Cafe in South Catlins, known for its delectable fresh cuisine and funky local arts and crafts, is always a must stop for Esther whenever she is visiting New Zealand's stunningly beautiful South Island.

Chapter 3

Meanwhile, Back at Old Bunbury

Clive Endive Ogive IV read Esther's text from New Zealand one more time. Like all of Esther's messages, it was exceedingly sincere and exceptionally well crafted. As much as he hated to admit, Clive was very much like Esther when it came to the fine art of preparing and delivering superior written communication. (Clive was loath to confess that he was like Esther in *anything*, although in the deepest recesses of his modern-day patrician mind, he knew this to be unarguably true.) Both Clive and Esther took great pains to make sure that *everything* they wrote was articulate, coherent, and syntactically and grammatically correct. Why in Jupiter's name should texting be any different? (LOL and WTF)

Clive was having lunch with three of his closest personal friends at the Old Bunbury Golf Links & Reading Club, the unquestionable favorite of the nineteen *very* exclusive and prestigious private clubs to which he proudly belonged. He and his friends were going to tee it up this glorious late-August afternoon after everyone had finished eating, and the longstanding quartet was very much looking forward to its usual afternoon of great camaraderie and mediocre golf. To Clive's immediate left sat J. Eaton Swank—Eat-o to his inner circle—a longtime Old Bunbury member currently serving out his sixth consecutive term as a member of the Board of Directors. Like Clive, Eat-o belonged to a good number of the world's most prestigious and exclusive private clubs. Unlike Clive, Eat-o was widely known and greatly respected among the closely knit community of high-end private club leaders as a person of unquestionable integrity, superior private-club knowledge, razor-sharp intellect, and extensive governance expertise. In other words, Eat-o was the walking and talking antithesis of the typical private club board member.

"It sure is nice and quiet without Esther around," Eat-o said to no one in particular between gentlemanly bites of his free-range chicken salad sandwich on toasted whole wheat with a small side of fresh fruit. More often than not, this was his preferred lunch whenever he dined at Old Bunbury. "I'd be lying if I said I missed her."

"You got that right," Dr. Art "Check My Pulse" Le Fever agreed with unbridled enthusiasm. He was seated to Eat-o's immediate left and directly across from Clive at the group's favorite four-top in the far corner of the main dining room. More Old Bunbury members than not made it a point to affectionately ask Art to "Check My Pulse" whenever they encountered him at the club in memory of the time the good dermatologist had mistakenly pronounced fellow Old Bunbury member Ed Neffers dead. Ed, as it turned out, had accidentally overdosed on his medication, and the resulting rapid drop in blood pressure had caused him to pass out at table fourteen in the main dining room. When Ed had suddenly popped up from the table, face smothered in mushy peas and garlicky mashed potatoes, he had caused quite a ruckus—to put it mildly—among everyone present. After all these years, Art had learned to take the ensuing good-natured ribbing in stride.

Art was currently wolfing down his lunch selection of choice—a chili dog smothered in onions—between deep and satisfying gulps of his second ice-cold Heineken. "You know, I hate it when Esther waits on me. Just hate it. Half the time, that crazy broad completely ignores what I order and instead brings me a god-dammed plate of chopped lettuce topped with a thimbleful of tuna salad. I just know she and my wife are in cahoots. What Esther brings me wouldn't fill up a snotty two-year-old. Guppy shit—unadulterated guppy shit!"

The fourth member of the quartet was Danny Bumbery. Danny, painfully shy around all but his closest friends, had the misfortune of once having far too much to drink at an

Old Bunbury annual spring formal. (Overindulging in adult beverages was highly unusual in Danny's prudish world.) Towards the end of that unforgettable evening, Danny, unbeknownst to those few still remaining at the dance, had wandered out of the clubhouse and promptly passed out in the center of the clubhouse front lawn, only to get thoroughly doused when the club's sprinkler system unexpectedly kicked on. His wife, Edith, had never been so embarrassed in her entire life as when, with the snickering help of the valets, she had been forced to unceremoniously load a still loaded, sopping-wet Danny into their Cadillac Eldorado and drive him home. From that day forward, Danny had been known to everyone at the club, both members and staff, as Tuxedo Man.

(It is worth noting that most every Old Bunbury member—at least those who had belonged for more than a few years—had earned a moniker of some sort. Most wore them with unabashed pride. The conferring and gracious acceptance of such monikers was an inherent and celebrated part of the club's unique history, tradition, and culture. In its way, it went to the very essence of what membership in a great private club is all about.)

"The club did the right thing paying for Esther's latest New Zealand adventure," Danny suddenly piped in, sending the conversation into a new direction. "After all, she did nail Alfie's killer. Without Esther's help, who knows how long it would have taken for the police to solve that heinous crime. They weren't making much progress until Esther stuck her overly inquisitive nose right into the middle of things and figured it all out."

"Yes, indeed, she did us all a huge favor," echoed Eat-o. "Those were some very dark days here at our normally halcyon club. I'm quite relieved and happy that everything has return to normal—whatever that may mean—on these hallowed grounds. So, Clive-man, when exactly are you heading down to New Zealand?"

Abruptly dropping the remnants of his chili dog, Art shot Clive a hard, inquisitive stare. Danny, whose typical noon repast was a bowl of hearty chicken noodle with precisely five whole-grain Nabisco premium saltine crackers, confirmed his similar surprise when the spoon he was holding plopped straight down into the half-consumed bowl of soup directly in front of him.

"*You* are going to New Zealand?" asked a dumbfounded Danny. "Why on earth would you do that, man? Did you forget? *Esther* is there."

"Relax, gentlemen. It's not a secret," answered Clive quietly. "I was going to fill you in on all the details later today during our round. You know that the Kaikoura Whaling & Sailing Club—our sister club in New Zealand, I might add, in case anyone at this table has had a sudden memory lapse—is hosting a special dinner in Esther's honor this coming Saturday night. Kaikoura's club president, Rutherford Sparnacle—better known as Rusty to close friends like me—asked me if I would attend. You guys *do* remember that I'm also a Kaikoura member, right? Anyway, Rusty knows that Esther and I are close." *Is* that *what we are?* "Rusty thought it would be a wonderful way to further honor Esther as well as allow me the opportunity to catch up with some old buddies down in Kaikoura. I thought it was an excellent suggestion, so I quickly agreed. I'm flying out tomorrow night."

"I remember Rusty," Eat-o chimed in. "He came with you to the annual member-guest a few years ago. Great guy! As I recall, he carried your sorry ass for all four days. Danny and Art, you remember him. Oh no, wait. You don't. You gentlemen—and I apply the term most generously—were both too cheap to invite guests that year. Anyway, when Clive asked me this morning what I thought of the idea, I told him that I very much supported his decision. Plus, you've got to admit, it's a classic win-win for all of us. The Clive-man gets to see some old pals at one of his preferred private clubs,

Esther gets to see her 'hero,' Clive—we all know that she'll be completely surprised and genuinely pleased—and Old Bunbury gets to savor the peace and quiet that will continue to reign supreme around here with both Clive and Esther gallivanting on the other side of the world."

"I don't know, Clive-man," said Danny, indecision clearly remaining in his voice. "We're talking about Esther, man. You know what they say about someone who might suddenly and unexpectedly be punched in the balls: Do not go genitally into that good right."

"You and your dumb-ass puns, Tuxedo Man," Art fired back, although he couldn't suppress the silly grin spreading across his face. (Gravitas was not the strongest asset of this particular group.) "Personally, I think it's a damn good idea. Eat-o got it exactly right, and our club president deserves everyone's full and unwavering support."

"You know, Tuxedo Man, you're always against everything," added Eat-o. "Hell, if you were a horse, you'd be the biggest neigh-sayer in this fearsome foursome," he deadpanned, looking directly at Danny, as he purposely stretched out the "neigh" to a high-pitched whinny. The mischievous twinkle in Eat-o's eyes was not lost on anyone at the table.

"It's a done deal, gentlemen," Clive said, bringing a welcome end to the burgeoning pun-fest. "I know you all will do your best to hold down the fort when I'm gone. To tell you the truth, I'm looking forward to a great trip," he added, getting up from his seat. "Besides, I think we all know that, deep down, Esther has a heart of gold."

"*Way* deep down," Danny qualified with a mischievous wink as he too stood. "Let's go play some golf."

Old Bunbury's Danny "Tuxedo Man" Bumbery is a significantly better punster and adult beverage imbiber than he is a golfer.

Chapter 4

Christchurch and the Journey Northward

Esther found herself once again standing behind the fluttering incandescent yellow tape demarcating the area that visitors were prohibited from entering. Beyond lay the devastated city center of Christchurch. She had been to this very same spot the day before last—a purposely chosen first stop on her eagerly anticipated whirlwind tour of greater Christchurch and the scenic environs of the surrounding Canterbury province—because from here she could catch a glimpse of the exact space where the magnificent historic Christchurch cathedral had once proudly ruled.

In her mind, the past forty-eight hours were racing helter-skelter: jam-packed, frenetic, and physically taxing, but to Esther, emotionally satisfying and intellectually stimulating as well. She began to smile as she relived her afternoon jaunt to Akaroa, the quaint resort town on the nearby wondrous Banks Peninsula renowned for its quirky shops, sheltered harbor, whale-watching boat outings, Gallic-named streets (reflecting its early days as a French settlement), diverse cuisine, and surrounding craggy, towering volcanic peaks. She had also re-driven the bulk of the spectacularly beautiful and, in places, tortuously winding famous Arthur's Pass road—one of the few "highways" on the South Island connecting the east and west coasts. Her journey had taken her through verdant patchwork farmland and as far as the historic Wobbly Kea cafe in the aptly named pristine Alpine outpost of Arthur's Pass, where she had treated herself to the smoked blue cod quesadilla special with a house salad and raspberry iced tea. But her wonderful Canterbury Province adventures had not been limited to the outdoors. She had also spent several intense and fascinating hours studying the interactive exhibits at the highly acclaimed International Arctic Centre adjacent to Christchurch International, where, in classic Esther style, she had driven herself to permanently absorb everything she could about the various species of penguins that populated New Zealand. (The Little Blue Penguins, a species that no longer bred near towns and cities, except for nearby Oamaru, remained her favorites.)

Now, Esther's farewell visit to remember and, in her own personal way, appropriately honor the famous Christchurch cathedral had caused the tears to come flooding back. The recently deconsecrated and essentially demolished old Christchurch Cathedral had been one of her favorite man-made landmarks in the entire country. The February 2011 earthquake, she knew, had killed close to two hundred New Zealanders, most all of them in central Christchurch, making it the second most deadly natural disaster in the country's recorded history. Although no one had died in the cathedral itself during that particular quake—at a 6.3 on the Richter scale, it was by far the most powerful and destructive—the massive damage, in combination with the destruction wrought by the earlier earthquake of September 2010 and its aftershocks, was simply too severe for the famed Anglican house of worship to long survive.

Esther fondly remembered her previous claustrophobic, arduous ascents—she'd done it on two separate occasions—up the cathedral spire's dank, narrow, circular stone staircase. Upon reaching the top, she had been rewarded with a panoramic view of Cathedral Square, all of downtown Christchurch, and, in the distance, the glistening Southern Alps, the snow-capped mountainous spine of the South Island. She thought it incredibly sad to realize that the original Christchurch Cathedral, in all its centuries of splendor and glory, would in due course fade into nothing more than a vague and distant memory. Reverently nodding her head one last time in humble tribute towards where the magnificent edifice to Christianity had once stood, Esther wiped away the last of her tears, turned, and strolled back to her double-parked Camry. Less than a half hour later, she was beyond the outskirts of the city and well into what promised to be a leisurely and enjoyable drive up the east coast towards Kaikoura.

Indeed, Esther took her merry old time, making several stops at particularly scenic points—for Esther, *all* of New Zealand was scenic, some places only more so than others—and one major serendipitous deviation en route. She didn't need to be in Kaikoura until Saturday afternoon, so she had the rest of today and, if necessary, all of tomorrow morning before she was scheduled to meet with the leaders of the Kaikoura Whaling & Sailing Club for her personalized guided tour of the club's facilities. That part of her visit would likely be both pleasant and interesting, she thought, but she was not particularly looking forward to the pomp and circumstance that would surely accompany the evening dinner in her honor. Trooper that she was, however, Esther would make the best of it, if only out of respect to her dear friend and longtime mentor President Clive.

Esther's first stop along Route 1 was in the fertile Waipara Valley at the highly acclaimed Pegasus Bay Winery and Restaurant, where she had been fortunate enough to have secured three bottles of Virtuoso, their top Chardonnay and a vintage that was only produced in exceptional growing seasons. *Hey, it never hurts have a few bottles of great Chardonnay on hand.* Esther was enough of an oenologist to know that wine-harvesting emergencies can and do happen.

Esther spent a full hour with Paul Donaldson, the youngest son of Pegasus Bay founder Ivan Donaldson and now general manager of the family-owned business. As they casually strolled the entire property, Paul provided Esther with a detailed update on how operations had evolved at Pegasus Bay since her last visit. According to Paul, the family had, like most of the other top New Zealand wineries, focused of late on the critical importance of sustainability. Paul told Esther that, from his family's perspective as successful viticulturalists, sustainability, at its core, meant "the capacity to endure and prosper by appropriately understanding, implementing, and embracing industry best practices in a safe, efficient, and environmentally friendly manner." Paul's wise words, to Esther's way of thinking, had made very good sense indeed.

"Thank you for everything, Paul. It was so good to see you again," Esther said, her gratitude obvious, as she prepared to take her leave, knowing that it would be rude to occupy any more of the general manager's valuable time.

"And you as well, Esther," Paul answered in his kindly manner. "Enjoy your Virtuoso. As you know, we rarely have it on hand, but I was more than happy to put away a few bottles for one of my favorite customers. Safe travels—and enjoy the rest of your stay. My family and I look forward to seeing you on your next visit to Aotearoa."

From there, purely on a whim, Esther hung a left onto the nearby Waipara Flat road—New Zealand Route 7—so she could make her way to Hanmer Springs, a small, out-of-the-way Alpine tourist village that she had somehow missed during all of her former New Zealand visits. Esther would make up for that unfortunate lapse now.

After exploring the town center—she felt vaguely unfulfilled when she had finished, perhaps, to be fair, because it was the off season and a good number of the shops and restaurants had not been open—Esther enjoyed a midafternoon meal at the historic Garden House Cafe, a dining establishment long known for its exclusive views over Hanmer Springs's picturesque thermal-pools complex. The Moroccan chicken salad, a house specialty, substantially exceeded her gustatory expectations.

Suddenly realizing she could still make Kaikoura by nightfall—one of Esther's rare, begrudging concessions to age was that she no longer ever drove after dark—she promptly returned to her car and pressed on. Esther knew that she didn't have all that far to go. She would simply backtrack on Route 7 until it intersected with Route 70. From there, she would head northeast through the breathtaking Seaward Kaikoura Range until she rejoined Route 1 for the short northerly drive directly into Kaikoura.

Her impromptu plan worked to perfection; Esther pulled into town just as the sun was beginning to disappear behind the glorious, snowcapped heights of Mount Tinline.

The magnificent Christchurch cathedral as it looked before the devastating South Island earthquakes of 2010 and 2011.

Chapter 5

Kaikoura

Esther "slept in" until just after seven on Saturday morning, a sinfully decadent hour at which to begin the day for someone so Spartan in her sleep habits. It was clear that the previous several days of whirlwind travel and nonstop activity had combined to take their toll. Esther had to admit to herself that, as exhausted as she had felt during last evening's excellent, if somewhat hurried, dinner—she'd had the featured roasted rolled lamb stuffed with garlic, rosemary, and heirloom tomatoes at her favorite Kaikoura restaurant, the Green Dolphin Restaurant and Bar, and was back in her room and fast asleep shortly after eight—the eleven hours of continuous, undisturbed rest had surely done her a world of good. Her overnight physical rejuvenation, in combination with the serenity that was steadily growing inside her, produced that welcome, comforting euphoria that never failed to materialize whenever she set foot on her beloved New Zealand soil.

Esther had come to accept, albeit with a reluctance approaching sheer obstinacy, the arthritis that was slowly, irreversibly further deforming her already gnarled fingers as well as the annoying—and, if she dwelt too long on it, downright scary—numbness that had permanently encamped in several of her bony toes. Travel, however, was an elixir, her own personal magical potion for mental and physical rejuvenation. And for Esther, travel to New Zealand was doubly potent in its restorative powers. Though Esther knew that New Zealand travel, in and of itself, did not and could not halt or reverse the growing ill effects of advancing age, she also knew its therapeutic effects did wonders to focus and sharpen her still inquisitive mind, improve her spirits, and allow her to discard, if only temporarily, the various and sundry ailments now affecting her increasingly frail body. New Zealand was Esther's fountain of youth.

Esther, now fully awake, washed and busily dressing for breakfast, once again congratulated herself for having had the good sense to have driven all the way to Kaikoura the previous afternoon. Doing so had allowed her to get the rest she had so obviously needed. Between her yet-to-be-planned morning activities, the afternoon tour of the Kaikoura Whaling & Sailing Club, and the evening's dinner and festivities in her honor, it was going to be another long and busy day.

Pulling into town the previous evening, Esther had correctly surmised that she would have her pick of places at which to stay the night. The first signs of spring had barely arrived this far south of the equator, and it would be three months before the hectic summer season was in full swing. Accordingly, she had immediately driven to the Anchor Inn Motel, a modern, luxurious accommodation located directly on the waterfront esplanade. She had stayed here, always with great satisfaction, many times in the past. In Esther's good judgment, no place offered higher quality amenities and friendlier service or had a better view of Kaikoura's majestic inland and seaward ranges.

"Esther! What a wonderful surprise!" Keith Hockney had beamed when Esther had walked into the modest motel office. Keith, along with his wife, Pauline, and fellow Kiwis Craig and Jacqui Whibley, had owned and managed the Anchor Inn for quite some time.

"It's great to see you as well, Keith. You know that whenever I come to Kaikoura, I *always* stay at the Anchor Inn."

"Yes, I do. However, I thought this time might be different, given the special circumstances that bring you here. Quite frankly, I just assumed that the Kaikoura Whaling & Sailing Club had made other lodging arrangements for you." Indeed, the good people at the Kaikoura Whaling & Sailing Club had repeatedly offered to put Esther up at one of their members' homes during the time she would be in town. Esther, however, had graciously but firmly declined. She had not known for certain exactly when she would be arriving, and more importantly, she utterly despised being beholden to anyone or being forced to adhere to someone else's schedule. Esther not only danced to her own drummer; she wrote her own music as well.

"How do you know about that?" Esther had asked, the temporary befuddlement obvious to Keith.

"Esther, Kaikoura is a small town," he had answered. "There are no secrets here. We all know about your heroic adventures back in the United States. Congratulations are certainly in order, and what better way than for our club to host a gala evening in your honor? Pauline and I, in fact, will be attending. We wouldn't miss it for the world."

"That's fantastic, Keith," Esther had responded, genuinely pleased at the show of support. "I just hope everyone doesn't make too much of a fuss. Now, if you don't mind, I'd like to check in. Hopefully, my favorite room, number 5, is unoccupied. I'm going to have a quick dinner and go to bed early. Tomorrow will be a long day."

On Saturday morning, Esther enjoyed a continental breakfast at nearby Fluke's Cafe—she loved its funky decor and historic location at the old Railway Station—during which time she cautioned herself to take it easy. Knowing that the afternoon and evening would be hectic, she purposely chose to limit her first day's tourist activities to visiting just two places.

Her first stop was at Point Kean. Less than two miles from the center of town, Point Kean marked the place where the road ended and the Peninsula Walkway, the trail encircling the beautiful Kaikouran spit of land jutting out to sea, began. It was, more often than not, the perfect spot to view a variety of marine mammals in their natural habitat, and she was not disappointed on this particular visit. On this unusually crisp morning, with the sun glistening in the crystal-clear sky and silhouetting the snowcapped mountains shimmering in the distance, Esther counted dozens of fur seals and seven albatross on the shoreline rocks and two dusky dolphins farther out to sea. Her patience was further rewarded when, less than a half hour later, she spotted a sperm whale about eighty yards offshore. (Humpback whales, orca, and the rare hector's dolphins, she knew, would not arrive until the warmer summer months.)

Esther tried to imagine the jumble of wondrous thoughts filling Captain Cook's mind when he had first seen the spectacularly beautiful and pristine Kaikouran Peninsula less than two hundred and fifty years ago. She knew that it hadn't taken all that long for other Europeans to follow, because by 1843, a small but permanent settlement had been established and the first full-fledged whaling station had been opened. The boom, however, had lasted less than three decades, as the unhealthy overfishing had caused the sperm and fluke population to decline to the point where whaling activities had become economically unprofitable. For the last century and a half, most people in Kaikoura had earned their livings by farming and fishing and, in more recent times, from the increasingly significant tourist dollars generated by sightseeing and ecotourism.

Esther's second stop was at the Kaikoura Historical Society District Museum & Archives. The small, modest building right off Route 1 on Ludstone Road meticulously documented the fascinating history of the area and also housed an extensive display of local Maori artifacts; old whaling, fishing, and farming implements; various and sundry social records; marine fossils; historic sepia photographs; and assorted archives of memorabilia that, taken together, had helped make Kaikoura what it was today. The fact that Esther had seen it all before did nothing to dampen her enthusiasm for today's return visit.

When she had finished with her encore museum tour, Esther grabbed a quick bite—broiled garlic scallops and a Coca-Cola—at Kaikoura Seafood BBQ, nothing more than an unpretentious shack situated roadside on Fyffe Quay. With its ever-changing daily specials hastily scribbled on old chalkboards, patrons savoring their food outdoors on roughhewn timber tables, seagulls cawing noisily in the background, and the alluring smell of fresh fish broiling on the barbie wafting through the salted air, it was easy to see why this dining establishment was a particular favorite of the local populace.

Just as Esther was finishing lunch, her iPhone 5 began to chirp, indicating that she had just received a text. It said, "Dear Esther: I am so happy to hear that you have arrived safely to our beautiful town. We very much look forward to seeing you at three this afternoon for your tour of the Kaikoura Whaling & Sailing Club and, in the evening, at the banquet in your honor. Sincerely, Rutherford Sparnacle, President."

Keith Hockney was right. There are no *secrets in a small town.* After a courteous response confirming that she would be at the club at three, Esther drove back to the Anchor Inn to prepare for the rest of the day.

Kaikoura, New Zealand—the little South Island town that has magically captured Esther's good-natured heart.

Chapter 6

Clive Arrives

Clive had arrived in Kaikoura on Friday afternoon as well, about two hours earlier than Esther. He had, however, taken an entirely different route from the United States, in part because he wanted to minimize the chances of accidentally bumping into Esther as she wandered north from Christchurch—Esther was living proof of the existence and accuracy of Murphy's Law—but mainly because he was a Delta guy. If a Delta jet, or one of Delta's good Sky Team partners, flew to where he was going (or, by air travel standards, "close by"), then that's who he went with. Period. From Clive's perspective, Delta surely wasn't perfect—he'd experienced the occasional airline snafus that were statistically bound to happen to anyone who'd traveled as much as he—but, all things considered, Clive still deemed the company the best in the business when it came to delivering consistent, high-quality customer service. Clive had flown Delta so often that he'd long ago reached the coveted Two Million Miler status, guaranteeing him Gold Medallion SkyMiles membership for life. A while back, he had even attained the lofty Platinum Medallion SkyMiles tier two years running—he had logged 145,000 and 157,000 Medallion Qualification Miles during those particularly hectic twenty-four months—primarily because of so many overnighters to Asia, Europe, and the Middle East.

Clive had taken Delta flight DL0017 from Los Angeles to Sydney's Kingsford Smith International—he flew Business Elite, of course—where he had then transferred to an Air New Zealand flight directly into Wellington. From there, after securing his Hertz rental car, Clive had boarded the famous Interislander Ferry for its morning departure across the choppy, windswept Cook Strait to Picton—a three-hour trip that he had made once before and found memorably exhilarating—and then made the leisurely one-hundred-mile drive south on Route 1 directly into Kaikoura.

Upon his arrival, Clive immediately drove to the beautiful contemporary home of his longtime friend and fellow Kaikoura Whaling & Sailing Club member Rusty Sparnacle, which was strategically situated atop the craggy bluff overlooking the town, the bay, the peninsula, and the distant Kaikoura ranges. Rusty had graciously offered to have Clive stay in his spacious guest suite during the time Clive would be in town.

The two old friends greeted each other warmly when Clive pulled into Rusty's driveway. "Clive-man, it's great to see you again, old buddy! It's been way too long. What, four years? You're looking fit and trim. Must be all that excellent food and service that your now-famous waitress par excellence provides for you at Old Bunbury."

"I haven't even unpacked and you're already giving me crappola about Esther," Clive replied with the endless good-natured kidding that typically exists between longtime great friends. (Well, male friends). "And it's been closer to five since we last saw each other, mate. Remember, you and Glenda stayed at my home the week of the Old Bunbury Annual Member Guest. Thanks to my unusually consistent ball-striking and superior putting, you and I finished second in our flight. I carried your sorry ass for four days straight. I still have the plaque hanging in my den."

"You're right, of course. Man, time does indeed fly. It'll be two years next month since I lost my dear Glenda. She suffered so much during that last six months. Pancreatic cancer is a bitch," Rusty said, his eyes beginning to mist over. "I still miss her."

"I'm sorry I couldn't make it to the funeral, my friend."

"As I've already told you several times, no worries in that regard. I completely understand. We live on completely opposite sides of the world. Now let me help carry your luggage to your room," Rusty said, changing the subject as he picked up the larger of Clive's two Eagle Creek suitcases. "After you get yourself situated, come on down and we'll sit on the deck, take in the view—it's a damn spectacular one, as I am sure you remember—catch up on life, and go over the plans for tomorrow evening. I'll have your Belvedere gimlet—it looks like you could use a double—ready and waiting."

Twenty-five minutes later, the two were sitting on Rusty's spacious veranda, silently enjoying the sunny, unseasonably warm late-afternoon weather and spectacular panorama in comfortable, peaceful silence. "You know, Clive-man, I never get tired of the view," Rusty said after a good ten minutes had passed, the appreciation apparent in his demeanor. "Never. We've both been all over the world and have seen some awesome sights and damn beautiful places, but to me, this is as good as it gets."

"You'll get no argument from me," Clive answered, nodding his head in agreement. "So, mate, fill me in on tomorrow's festivities."

"Well, it looks we'll have about fifty people, give or take, for dinner, including several Kaikoura club officers and board members. Remember, this is the off season, and most of our members are still out of town. We'll have a small head table of five—you, Esther, me, and Keith and Pauline Hockney, Esther's friends who own the Anchor Inn Motel in town. We're keeping it simple—a nice, well-paced three-course dinner followed by just two speakers, you and me, and then we'll conclude with a few words from Esther herself. We both know how much Esther hates pomp and circumstance. Hell, you and I despise it too."

"All sounds good," Clive readily agreed.

"Clive, just so you know, the board voted unanimously to make Esther an honorary member of our club. We both know how much she *loves* all things New Zealand, and Kaikoura in particular, and we think it's a wonderful way for the Whaling & Sailing Club to appropriately recognize and honor her Old Bunbury heroics. I'll make the announcement tomorrow evening; I'm sure it will make her proud and happy. Anyway, it won't be all that long before Esther's too damn old to travel. You and I, my friend, are nearing that very same stage of life. By the way, I completely understand Old Bunbury's decision not to do the same; Esther still works for you—if you can call it that," Rusty finished with a wry smile.

"I agree that there's got to be a better word for what she does at Old Bunbury," Clive answered. "More accurate to say that she shows up *if* she wants, *when* she wants, and, *if* the mood strikes, waits on *whomever* she wants in *whatever* manner she wants. It's no coincidence that our good club manager, Jay Morris—you remember Jay, I'm sure, from the Member-Guest—has now gone completely gray in what little hair he has remaining because he has to deal with Esther on a regular basis."

"Please extend my deepest sympathies to Jay when you get back home," Rusty answered, a wry smile creeping across his face. "Anyway, Clive, that's the general plan, and we think it's a good one. If I know you—and, fortunately or unfortunately, I do—I'm sure you concur. The very best part of the day, of course, will be when Esther walks through the front door of the clubhouse tomorrow afternoon. I can't wait to see the startled look that will surely cross her face when she sees *you.*" His amusement turned into outright laughter. "It's going to be a moment none of us will ever forget."

"That's for damned sure, my friend."

"Now let me get you a refill on that Belvedere gimlet. I could use another Speight's Gold Medal, the best ale this side of paradise. I've got a Caesar salad and a large pizza coming at six thirty—onions, jalapenos, and extra cheese, just the way you like. Neither of us is leaving this house for any reason until tomorrow afternoon. We're not taking *any* chances of having Esther spot you."

Cognizant of the fact that Rutherford "Rusty" Sparnacle is a consistently weak slicer, the neighboring sheep no longer pay much attention when he tees off.

Chapter 7

The Kaikoura Whaling & Sailing Club

Esther arrived at the tastefully understated entrance to the Kaikoura Whaling & Sailing Club at precisely four minutes to three. The trip, if you could call it that, had taken her all of eleven minutes, and she had unluckily missed both traffic lights. Un-Estherlike, she had spent the previous half hour meticulously grooming herself for what she knew would be a very special occasion. (Ever fastidious with regard to personal attire, at a critically important sartorial time such as this, Esther preferred St. John Knits for its mature simplicity, chic comfort, and classic confidence of style.) Esther was, in her way, "officially representing" Old Bunbury, her favorite private club in the entire world, and she wanted to be at her very best.

Esther knew, of course, that the Whaling & Sailing Club was the very prestigious and highly exclusive New Zealand sister club to Old Bunbury. She also was well aware of the fact that its longtime president, Rutherford Sparnacle—someone whom she, quite correctly, deemed a gentleman of indubitable class and unblemished integrity—was a great personal friend of President Clive and had once been his designated invitee to the Old Bunbury Annual Member-Guest. Other than that, her knowledge of the Whaling & Sailing Club—its membership, amenities, facilities, history, traditions, and culture—was minimal. She had once, by pure happenstance, driven past the entrance to the club on a previous visit to Kaikoura but, at the time, had neither a desire nor a reason to enter and learn more. Her forthcoming tour, about which she had once been fretting, might very well turn out to be an interesting and enjoyable adventure after all.

Uncharacteristically, Esther checked herself in the Camry's rearview mirror one last time—although a lot of things, Esther was not typically one to preen—got out of the car, closed the door, and strode resolutely towards the front entrance of the clubhouse. Just as she was about to enter, the massive weathered solid-oak door began to slowly creak outward. There, arms akimbo and with a broad, welcoming smile spanning his handsome, weathered face, stood Rutherford Sparnacle.

"Esther, it is so nice to see you again. On behalf of our entire membership, it is my special pleasure and honor to welcome you to the Kaikoura Whaling & Sailing Club," Rusty Sparnacle said with all the grace and dignity befitting his critically important position at so distinguished an institution. "Please, do come in."

"Thank you so much, Mr. Sparnacle. Please let me say, first off, that I was so sorry to hear about the passing of your beautiful wife, Glenda. I thoroughly enjoyed meeting the both of you five years ago at Old Bunbury. She was a loving and classy woman."

"Thank you, Esther. Indeed, she was."

"And how are your two fine sons, Rutherford Junior and Sedgemore, doing? When you and I were last together, young Rutherford was flourishing in his junior year at Dunedin's acclaimed University of Otago—majoring in Chinese anthropology, as I recall—and Sedgemore was excelling in his first-year studies at the world-renowned Auckland Law School. I also recollect that both young men were excellent musicians and accomplished rugby players as well."

"Your memory is as razor sharp as ever, Esther. No wonder you were so monumentally successful in your now-famous sleuthing activities at Old Bunbury. Both of my sons are doing quite well, thank you. Rusty Junior is now married to Glynnis; has a beautiful two-year-old daughter, Gwendolyn; and lives and works in Wellington. Sedgemore is seriously dating a wonderful young lady, Prissy MacDougal from Invercargill, and is successfully practicing law at Russell McVeagh."

"Ah, New Zealand's most highly regarded law firm," Esther said. "Please pass on my best to both young men. True chips off the old block."

"Indeed I will, Esther. Thank you. And now, if you don't mind, I'd like to tell you a little bit about today's schedule of activities. I will be your personal guide for this afternoon's tour. In a moment, we will be joined by another gentleman who will eagerly accompany us on our stroll around these hallowed grounds. Once we've finished, you are free to go back to the Anchor Inn for a bit of a rest before this evening's dinner, which will commence promptly at seven. Please rest assured that, in accordance with your well-documented personal desires, we will be keeping the formalities to a minimum. I personally share your disdain for pomp and circumstance and, also like you, purposely eschew the limelight whenever possible. We should finish up no later than nine thirty."

"Thank you, sir," Esther said. "That all sounds wonderful. And who will be accompanying us when you show me around the club? Do I know this gentleman?"

"Ah, the essence of our dear Esther—ever inquisitive, unflinchingly candid, and straight to the point. Well, it's time to welcome the third member to our peripatetic trio—someone you do indeed know quite well." And, just as Rusty Sparnacle finished speaking, Clive entered the foyer.

Clive had seen and learned a *lot* about Esther over the years, but one thing he had never seen or known her to be was speechless—until now. It took Esther a full ninety seconds before she was able to finally blurt out, with tears of joy streaming down her reddened cheeks, "*Boss*, what in the world are *you* doing here?"

"Isn't it obvious, Esther? I'm here to help you celebrate your big day at the Kaikoura Whaling & Sailing Club," Clive beamed. "When my good friend and fellow private club president Rusty asked me to attend and participate, there was no possible way I could turn him down. It is truly my pleasure and honor to be here with you for what surely will be a momentous and memorable event for all of us."

"Boss, I don't know what to say, other than thank you, thank you, *thank you*!" Esther gushed. "This, I now know, is going to be one of the best days of my entire life. I'm in my favorite town in my favorite country—other than the good old US of A, of course—with two of the finest people in the entire world. Life just doesn't get any better!"

"See, Clive, I told you your being here wasn't such a bad idea after all," Rusty deadpanned, looking directly at his good friend. The three began to laugh aloud.

"That you did, mate. That you did," Clive added after catching his breath. "I'd say it's time for us to get on with the tour."

For the next hour, the blissfully happy trio roamed the entire club property, as Rusty proudly identified and carefully described the various facilities and amenities while intermittently narrating the club's long and storied history.

"The Whaling & Sailing Club is one hundred seventy-four years old, Esther," Rusty began. "Interestingly, no one at the club has had anything to do with the whaling industry for well over a century. One of these days, our Board of Directors may actually get around to addressing the issue of our outdated, perhaps even politically incorrect, name, but I wouldn't count on that happening anytime soon."

"There are private clubs all over the world whose names no longer accurately describe the current status of the club, if they ever did," Clive chimed in; his encyclopedic knowledge of the myriad eccentricities of the zany world of private clubs was unmatched. "Consider," he continued, "the

Lakeland Yacht & Country Club in central Florida, a fine establishment that for many years now has offered its members neither yachting nor golf. Or what about the esteemed White Bear Yacht Club in White Bear Lake, Minnesota, a beautiful eastern suburb of the Twin Cities? That particular club's most valued asset, other than the members and staff, of course, is its beautiful and meandering Donald Ross-designed golf course. You certainly can't tell *that* from the club's official name."

"No you can't," Rusty heartily agreed. "While we do offer our members sailing, as our club name indicates, we also have one of the most challenging, meticulously maintained eighteen holes to be found anywhere in New Zealand, if not the entire southern hemisphere. Clearly, the Whaling & Sailing Club's official name gives no clue whatsoever to the existence of an unarguably world-class golfing venue on these cherished ninety-three hectares."

His oratorical momentum building, Rusty proudly pressed on. "Our membership roster, Esther, includes distinguished locals as well as civic, political, and business leaders from all over New Zealand and eleven foreign countries spanning the globe. Indeed, a previous Board of Directors, in a rare and blatant lapse in good judgment, blessed Clive's joining our select fold," he added, his hazel eyes affixed on his great friend from the United States.

"I suspect that the membership committee may, at some point, wish to revisit that dubious decision," Clive opined. "However, as we three know, it is indeed the wise person who can toot his own horn without blowing it."

"Other amenities, Esther, include an understated whist, cribbage, and canasta center; lawn bowls; croquet; and two separate dining rooms, the smaller of which, as you saw, is in dire need of attention," Rusty quickly continued, grimacing in a futile attempt to ignore Clive's infamous droll attempt at humor. (As a loyal and avid follower of @Clivethe-

ClubGuy—Clive's Twitter moniker—Rusty knew full well that his great friend was prone to interjecting subtle, or not-so-subtle, humor into any conversation wherever, whenever, and however he could.)

"Like Old Bunbury," Rusty added, "we eschew tennis, wellness facilities, and swimming pools and have neither the need nor desire for membership application forms, waiting lists, or marketing materials. If we want you to be a member, you will find out in due course. We have no presence whatsoever, we believe, on the World Wide Web and diligently strive to keep it that way. The bottom line is that we wish to remain off everyone's—and I do mean *everyone's*—radar, as far as such a thing is humanly possible."

"Now I understand why Old Bunbury and the Whaling & Sailing Club are sister clubs," Esther said."What a wonderful match!"

"Indeed!" Clive and Rusty answered in perfect unison, chuckling at their mutual social faux pas.

Having made their way back to the front entrance of the club, Rusty asked, "So, Esther, *that* is the Kaikoura Whaling & Sailing Club. Is there anything else you would like to see or know at this time?"

"No thank you, Mr. Sparnacle. Your guided tour has been comprehensive and fascinating. I truly appreciate your taking your valuable time to show me around this wonderful property. Your immense pride in the Kaikoura Whaling & Sailing Club is both obvious and justified. Now, if you and my boss will kindly excuse me, I want to head back to the Anchor Inn. It wouldn't look good, not good at all, having the guest of honor attend tonight's dinner with mascara streaking down her face."

Esther snapped this predawn shot of Kaikoura Bay standing directly across the street from the Anchor Inn Motel.

Chapter 8

The Gala Appreciation Dinner

Esther's celebratory evening, as it turned out, was a smashing success on all counts. The decorations were tasteful and apropos to the occasion. The food, everyone readily agreed, was superbly prepared, artfully arranged, and professionally delivered in a timely, courteous manner. Even Esther, qua waitress extraordinaire, was suitably impressed. (Okay, "waitress extraordinaire" may be a bit of an exaggeration when it comes to Esther, but to be fair, most of the people in attendance were sufficiently unfamiliar with her shall we say, "myriad eccentricities and peccadilloes" with regard to the necessities and nuances of extraordinary culinary service. They had, like far too many American voters in the 2012 presidential election, confused vacuous popularity with presumed expertise.) The attendees were also most gracious in welcoming Esther to the Kaikoura area. One of the local merchants even presented her with a sea-foam blue and snow-white "Esther loves Kaikoura and Kaikoura loves Esther" customized T-shirt. Most everyone stopped by Esther's table at some point during the evening to welcome her to the Whaling & Sailing Club as well as to offer assorted congratulatory comments on her now famous sleuthing exploits back in the United States. Most importantly, the speechifying was kept mercifully short. The only uncomfortable moment in the entire evening was Esther's brief but seemingly uncontrollable bout of sobbing for joy when Rusty, on behalf of the Board of Directors, thoroughly shocked her with an honorary lifetime membership in the club. However, she rallied nicely by delivering an articulate, heartfelt acceptance speech that was enthusiastically received by everyone in the room. By nine fifteen, every guest had gone save for

Rusty, Clive, Keith and Pauline Hockney, and the exceedingly grateful but emotionally spent guest of honor.

"Keith and Pauline, thank you so very much for coming," Esther said one last time to her favorite Kaikoura hoteliers as they were heading out the door. "I won't be long out of bed. I'm not sure how long I will be staying in town, but I will let you know something tomorrow. You two, as hard-working and talented innkeepers, know better than most that advance planning is not exactly my forte. And, as we all are well aware, there is a *lot* to see in this beautiful country of yours."

"You are most welcome, Esther. It was our honor and pleasure to spend such a memorable evening with you. We'll see you in the morning. Sleep well," Pauline said for the both of them.

"So, boss, how long are you staying in New Zealand?" Esther asked once the two friendly motel owners had gone.

"Rusty and I are leaving first thing in the morning for Cape Kidnappers," Clive said, not directly answering her question. "Our mutual good friend Tom Doak designed a spectacularly beautiful and challenging golf course up in Hawke's Bay on an especially beautiful portion of its emerald-green pasturelands overlooking the crashing whitecaps of the chilly South Pacific—but I am quite certain you already know all about that. You remember Tom, Esther. You met the legendary golf course architect at Old Bunbury several years ago when he partnered with Eat-o in our Annual Member-Guest. Anyway, Rusty and I are really looking forward to our trip; we have a lot of catching up to do. In my humble opinion, while Cape Kidnappers is no Old Bunbury nor Whaling & Sailing Club, it is arguably one of the very best signature layouts by a contemporary golf course designer on this good planet earth."

"Yes, I remember when Mr. Swank played with Mr. Doak. It was in 2010. They finished a solid third in the championship flight. In Friday's round, Mr. Swank powered a six iron through the gusting winds to nearly ace number seven," Esther recited, still infallible in all things Old Bunbury. "I've never been on the Cape Kidnappers golf course nor inside the resort's rustic lodge, boss, but I agree that the scenery in the Hawke's Bay and the Napier area is as awe-inspiring as it gets. On a previous trip, I spent several enjoyable hours touring the Mission Estate Winery, New Zealand's oldest, in the nearby Taradale Hills. Then again, as we three know only too well, one would be hard pressed to name *any* part of New Zealand that isn't breathtakingly beautiful."

"That's for sure, Esther," Clive readily agreed. Then, responding to her original query, he said, "After golf, I'll be heading straight home. You know that I can't stand to be away from Old Bunbury for too long. I don't want any overzealous directors messing things up in my absence," he said with an accompanying conspiratorial wink. "A few of them still think they know more about club management that our talented, time-tested general manager, Jay Morris—and I know you know exactly about whom I am speaking. Why is it so difficult for some board members to stick to their areas of responsibility—governance and strategic planning—and leave the day-to-day operations in the good hands of the paid professionals?" Clive lamented.

"Sorry, Esther. My train of thought got temporarily derailed," Clive said, refocusing on the conversation at hand. "What about you? How long will you be staying in Kaikoura?"

"Not sure, boss. As you know, I don't fly home until a week from tomorrow. I'm going to play it by ear." For Esther, while there surely were more than a few times when the subsequent "mowing" had turned out to be more problematic than she had expected, the grass truly was *always* greener on the other side of the fence.

As the happy trio left the building together and headed for their cars, Esther addressed both men one last time. "Gentlemen, I know that hugging and kissing aren't among our strong suits, and as much as I detest grammatical sloppiness and trite aphorisms, sometimes 'you just gotta do what you gotta do.' Besides, since no one else is around, I can always adopt Obama's laughable ploy after the 2012 Benghazi fiasco and claim plausible deniability," she said with a wry smile. "Then again, if they put someone in jail for blatant arrogance and gross stupidity, that guy would be serving a no-parole life sentence," Esther added as an afterthought. Her acerbic political commentary finished (for the time being), Esther gave them both a warm hug and then, tiptoeing, she brushed each man's left cheek with a gentle, affectionate kiss.

"Thank you both for your part in what has surely been one of the best days of my entire life," she gushed. "I will never, ever forget this day. Now before I start crying again, I'm going to take my leave and head down to the Anchor Inn and get some sleep. You two have a great golf getaway."

"And you enjoy the rest of your travels in New Zealand, Esther, " Clive said, also working hard to keep his emotions in check. "I'll see you back at Old Bunbury. Don't do anything I wouldn't do."

"That leaves it wide open, boss," Esther chuckled. "And Mr. Sparnacle," Esther added, looking directly at the Whaling & Sailing Club's talented and caring president, "the very best of everything to you and your wonderful family. It was truly a pleasure spending the afternoon and evening with you, and I am confident that our paths will cross again."

It would happen far sooner than either of them knew.

The lucky members of the Kaikoura Whaling & Sailing Club enjoy this spectacular view from the sixteenth tee.

Chapter 9

On the Road Again

Ever her restless, spontaneous self, Esther decided after an early Sunday-morning continental breakfast at Fluke's cafe that she would get into her car and, well, just drive. (Though the coffee and freshly baked Danish were, as usual, superbly prepared and promptly served, it was, of course, the unmatched views of the first hint of morning's glorious grey-orange hues behind the majestic Kaikoura Ranges that had been the real attraction.) Now that she was a semi-celebrity in the town—*Was* that *what she was?*—Esther knew herself well enough to realize that she didn't want to spend her valuable and limited New Zealand tourist time in idle chitchat with people who might now "recognize" her, stop her, and, God forbid, perhaps even pester her for an autograph, no matter how friendly and well intentioned virtually all of those good people would surely be. No, better to keep moving; there was much to do and see in her beautiful Aotearoa. Kaikoura, in all its splendor and beauty, would, no doubt, be alive and well when she next returned.

After Esther had gone back to her room, neatly packed her suitcases, and carefully stowed them in the Camry's good-sized trunk (aka, for non-American readers, the boot), she sauntered to the motel office to offer her fond farewells, as she had promised the previous evening, to Keith and Pauline. Because it was still quite early, however, neither had, understandably so, yet arrived. Accordingly, Esther composed a courteous thank-you note and slipped it, along with her old-fashioned metal room key, into an envelope taken from her room's stationary-and-postcard packet and slid it into the darkness under the office door. Keith and Pauline, nice people that they were, would surely understand, even appreciate, her spur-of-the-moment decision to press on.

After nearly an hour on the road—she had somehow found herself heading south on Route 1 at a unhurried but steady pace, stopping several times to visually drink in and savor the spectacular Pacific coastline—Esther decided, on pure whim, that the next major town that she would set her peripatetic sights upon would be Queenstown. (For Esther, touring her beloved New Zealand might best be described as one continuous, near-feverish attempt to permanently record, for later happy recall, all that she could successfully cram into her considerable long-term episodic memory.) As it turned out, in typical Esther fashion, the exact route that she would end up taking to the southern hemisphere's acknowledged premier four-season lake and alpine resort gave new meaning to circuitous.

When Esther came to Route 7, she turned right, taking the road's meandering northwesterly route as it began the torturous, occasionally downright scary, ascent through the awe-inspiring, snow-dusted mountain passes towards the coastal town of Greymouth, the South Island's largest port on the shimmering Tasman Sea. For reasons unknown, the remote intersection of Route 7 and Route 65—in and of itself nothing more than a nondescript spot in the middle of nowhere—had serendipitously reminded her of something that she had always wanted to do in New Zealand but, for whatever reason or reasons, had somehow failed to accomplish on all her previous visits: traverse the Buller Gorge swingbridge. Accordingly, Esther reprogrammed her mental map yet again and headed north on Route 65 until it intersected with Route 6. From there, it was a short twenty-minute drive northeast through Fern Flat to the low-key, rustic entrance to the attraction. (For many people, Esther's wanderings for the day would have constituted more than enough exploration for any given twenty-four–hour period, yet when she pulled into the parking lot, it was only eleven twenty in the morning. The day was still young.)

The scene of catastrophic floods, ground-rattling earthquakes, and devastating mudslides, the Buller River near Murchison, and the deep gorge its raging waters had methodically gouged over countless millennia, had been largely unexplored by Europeans until gold was discovered nearby in the middle of the nineteenth century. The Buller Gorge swingbridge, New Zealand's longest all–rope-and-board ravine-crossing structure at just over one hundred ten yards, was a relatively recent addition to the still-remote area, soaring majestically above the ever-rushing Buller River's turbulent and dangerous flow.

Esther found the walk across the swingbridge truly exhilarating. This particular v-shaped structure was made of multiple intricately woven ropes, with weathered pine slats serving as the narrow footpath and thick, waist-high, parallel polypropylene cords for its handholds. As she crossed, Esther could see and feel the seemingly flimsy structure sway in the gentle breeze, an unnerving motion that, ironically, was exacerbated by her very own cautious steps. The swiftly flowing waters below added to the disquieting illusion of the apparent precariousness of the structure, even as Esther's left brain constantly reassured her that the crossing would be perfectly safe.

Once on the other side—the thrilling transit had taken all of seven minutes—Esther strolled the easy loop on the densely forested peninsula trail, intensely studying the many information panels along the way that documented both the gold mining era and the significant destruction wrought by the 1929 Murchison earthquake. By the time she had made an equally inspiring return crossing and gotten back to her car, Esther knew that the "detour" to cross New Zealand's most famous rope bridge had been well worth the extra time and effort on her part. (Esther, in fact, understood far better than most that a good portion of life's best adventures and ensuing most treasured memories are those that are spontaneous and unplanned.)

It took Esther a little over three hours to make the hundred-mile journey from the Buller River Gorge into Greymouth, a leisurely drive that included three sightseeing pullovers and one short stop at a small, sparsely stocked rural grocery store to purchase a Diet Coke and the makings for a roast beef on rye. She had purposely taken the inland route for Greymouth for three reasons: It was fifteen miles shorter; she had, up until now, never travelled this particular way; and, most importantly, it had occurred to her that, on the following day, she could easily make—and also avoid the undesirable need to backtrack—the beautiful forty-minute drive up the west coast on Route 6 to revisit the Punakaiki Pancake Rocks and Blowholes, hidden gems that, to Esther's way of thinking, were as unique and mind-boggling natural wonders as any she had ever experienced. (New Zealand's rugged terrain, limited highways, and sparse population make the avoidance of at least a modicum of backtracking virtually impossible if one wishes to thoroughly explore the countryside.)

Weighing her options, Esther chose the Coleraine Motel for her night's lodgings, ideally situated on High Street and a scant two-minute drive from the Greymouth city center. She had stayed there once before and remembered how much she had enjoyed the motel's tastefully decorated guest lounge, replete with plush leather sofas, roaring fireplace, and large flat-screen television. With the innkeeper's assistance, she would find someplace nearby for a suitable evening repast, return to enjoy the amenities of the common area and her well-appointed room, and then, as was her custom, retire shortly after nine.

As part of her nightly ritual, Esther located her shiny new iPhone 5 and conscientiously plugged it in; she was meticulous about beginning each and every day with her cell fully charged. Mildly surprised to discover her phone off, Esther quickly remembered that she had purposely turned the communication device off the previous evening and left it in the car before entering the Whaling & Sailing Club. (Though Esther wasn't much for rules of *any* kind, even she could appreciate the untainted irony in the fact that, when it came to rules involving *another* private club—Old Bunbury, her home club, was another matter, of course—she *always* erred on the side of caution. Because Esther hadn't known the Whaling & Sailing Club's specific policies and procedures with regard to cell-phone usage on club premises, she had dutifully powered her phone down and temporarily stowed it in the Camry's otherwise empty glove compartment.)

Esther decided, as it was only eight forty-five, to turn her phone back on for a quick scan of the assorted e-mails, texts, and voice messages that would surely be awaiting her attention. She hadn't been expecting anything of importance. *I'm not a neurosurgeon on call; I'm a waitress on vacation from my job on the other side of the world. Who of importance could or would possibly want or need to speak with me?* Then again, perhaps she had won the Nigerian lottery—yet again. Accordingly, Esther was flabbergasted to see that she had two e-mails, three texts, and five voice messages, all from one person: her boss! *What in the world could* that *be about?*

Listening to and reading Clive's ten correspondences in the order in which they had been sent, Esther grew more ashen with each passing minute.

The Buller Gorge swingbridge and adjacent zip line soar majestically above the ever-rushing Buller River's turbulent and dangerous flow.

Chapter 10

Troubling News

"Hi, boss. It's me," were the first four monosyllables out of her mouth when Clive, recognizing the number, had immediately answered Esther's telephone call. Clive, in fact, was on the line and listening intently before Bobby Fuller had uttered a single word. (As his good friends and loyal Twitter followers well know, Clive's ringtone, for as long as he's had the ability to customize it, features the first several bars of the Bobby Fuller Four's timeless 1960s classic "I Fought the Law." July 18, 1966—the date Robert Gaston "Bobby" Fuller was discovered dead in the front seat of his car, the specific circumstances of that mysterious death unconfirmed to this very day—remains a sad memory for avid rock-and-roll fans everywhere.)

"Esther! Where in the world *are* you? I've been trying to get in touch with you all day! Are you alright?" came Clive's frantic response.

"Of *course* I'm alright, boss. Why would you ask *that*? And, as you know full well, I am right here in beautiful New Zealand. Specifically, I am now in the friendly port town of Greymouth, the terminus of the historic TranzAlpine Express, on the dramatic west coast of the South Island. I decided, on the spur of the moment, to leave Kaikoura early this morning. I just didn't have the heart to deal with all those people who might recognize me from last night's dinner. This fame thing isn't all it's cracked up to be. Deep down, boss, I am a very private person—exactly like you, I don't need to add."

"Why didn't you answer your cell? Wasn't it working properly? Were the batteries dead?" Clive pressed, although his voice was beginning to regain its regular pitch now that Esther appeared to be her normal self—whatever that might mean.

"Oh, that. I turned it off before last night's dinner at the Whaling & Sailing Club and stashed it in my rental car. I just now remembered to switch the thing back on. You know me—I'm paranoid about breaking *any* rules at another private club." *Okay, at Old Bunbury, I* do *tend to be a bit more flexible with regard to the policies and procedures.* "Anyway, boss, what's going on? I've been wading through your correspondence and getting more and more worried. Each one of your messages was more insistent than the last. So now I am doing what you repeatedly asked—calling you."

"I don't know how to break the news to you other than just come straight out with it. Adam Giztips, the good detective whom you helped identify Alfie Johnson's murderer—actually, it's probably more accurate to say that *he* assisted *you*—called this morning with some disturbing information. Very disturbing indeed. Hamish P. Tumorington, the former Old Bunbury member whom you and Adam nabbed for Alfie's despicable crime, just broke out of jail. He's on the loose, Esther!"

"Why didn't Detective Giztips call me directly? Surely, he must still have my cell number somewhere. Back then, he and I were speaking on almost a daily basis," Esther said.

He probably deleted it faster than Obama can issue another unconstitutional executive order. "A fair question, Esther. Adam told me he thought that, given your and my 'long-standing relationship'—I guess that accurately describes what you and I have—I would be the best one to let you know," Clive answered. Saying it aloud sounded just plain weird. He and Esther had a long-standing relationship?

"Fair enough, boss. Detective Giztips was indeed correct on that score. Still, I don't understand the escalating sense of urgency in your messages. We're both in New Zealand, for heaven's sake. Mr. Tumorington is on the other side of the world."

"Actually, Esther, no one knows *where* Hamish is at the moment. An intense manhunt is, as I understand it, already well underway, but so far, he has been successful in eluding his many pursuers. It's as if Hamish has vanished into the proverbial thin air," Clive said. "And there's more, Esther," he added, the hesitancy clear in his voice.

"Tell me, boss. I'm a big girl. I can handle it," Esther said, trying hard to control the rising snippet of panic inside her.

"A threatening note was found in his empty cell, Esther—a correspondence, it is clear, that Hamish purposely left behind for the guards and police to see. It says, and I quote, 'Tell that crazy old busybody I'm coming after her. I'm going to get even if it's the last thing I ever do. When I'm finished, Esther, if she's admitted—something about which I have serious doubts—will be a permanent resident of the great private club in the sky.'"

Hamish P. Tumorington, who *always* referred to himself as Hamish P. Tumorington—nothing more and nothing less, and *never* ignoring or dropping the *P.*—had been a relatively little known Old Bunbury member before the tragedy had occurred. To most, even now, he remained an enigma. In a fit of rage, most probably the result of spiraling gambling debts and the uncontrolled jealousy resulting from his perceived snub by the Old Bunbury Golf Links & Reading Club's prestigious Pillow Committee, Hamish had brutally murdered his fellow member/personal-bookie/fellow Pillow-Committee aspirant, Alfie Johnson. Esther, with her encyclopedic knowledge of all things Old Bunbury, had been instrumental in his quick arrest and timely conviction. It was painfully clear that Hamish was now hell-bent upon revenge.

"Well, *that's* certainly not anything I want to hear," Esther said, attempting to downplay what was obviously unsettling news. "But I'll say it again, boss. You and I are in New Zealand and we *know* Hamish is not. Even if he were to come here—and I think that is nothing more than fanciful speculation at this point—it would still be close to three days before it were even theoretically possible for him to set foot on New Zealand soil. We both know that it is a *long* flight here from the States, assuming he could even get past airport security." *Wait, I take that back. The Transportation Security Administration makes other federal bureaucracies look competent and efficient.* "And there is that time-change thing, boss. Remember, New Zealand is fourteen hours ahead of us," Esther added for good measure.

"You are, of course, correct on all counts. I am more worried about what might happen when you get back to the States. Despite being a convicted murderer, Hamish still has a *lot* of influential connections from his days at Old Bunbury. And don't forget, Esther, he isn't exactly lacking when it comes to creativity and financial resources. To put it bluntly, Hamish is free, well-connected, rich, smart, and on a mission of vengeance."

"Let's deal with all that when we both return, boss. For the time being, I don't want to hear any more about it," Esther said, the finality in her voice unmistakable. Changing the topic, she asked, "So, boss, how's Cape Kidnappers?"

"It's beautiful, of course, but neither Rusty nor I played very well today. As you can imagine, we've been preoccupied with the escape as well as our frantic efforts to get in touch with you. And Esther, before we get completely off topic, you and I *will* deal with the Hamish issue in an appropriate manner when you get home. I will *not* allow your life to be put in danger. Let's just hope the police are successful in their quest before then," Clive added.

"Thanks, boss. You do know how much I appreciate and value your friendship and support. However, I think it wise that we both do our best to put all of this out of our minds for now and try to enjoy our remaining time in New Zealand. When we get back to the good old US of A, we'll figure out our next steps."

"Fair enough, Esther," Clive agreed.

"And boss," Esther added. "I suggest you tell Detective Giztips that you and I have spoken and that I am just fine. He may be a bit of a fuddy-duddy and a worrywart, but Detective Giztips is also a quite competent policeman and a very nice man. He and I can and will catch up when I get home."

"I'll speak with him," Clive said amicably.

"Now if you don't mind, we both should get some much-needed rest. It's been a long and exhausting day. I've still got *lots* of places to see and things to do here in my beloved Aotearoa, and only nine days remaining before my plane leaves for home. I *promise* that I will give you a call or send you a text if I hear or need anything," she concluded.

"Sounds good, Esther. Try not to worry. My educated guess is that the police will capture Hamish sooner rather than later. That vile murderer deserves to be behind bars for the rest of his wretched life."

"Indeed he does, boss. Indeed he does. Good night," Esther said, signing off.

Hamish P. Tumorington, the convicted murderer of Alfie Johnson, on the day he was booked for his heinous crime.

Chapter 11

On the Lam

Hamish P. Tumorington, with his room's solid-oak door double-locked and old-fashioned brass latch chain securely fastened, cautiously inched back the floor-length opaque mauve linen drapes shrouding his hotel's window from the outside world. Three millimeters of eyeball space was all he needed to systematically, inconspicuously scan the tranquil courtyard below. He neither saw nor, more importantly, sensed anything out of the ordinary. An involuntary, near-imperceptible, sigh of relief escaped his haggard face. It appeared that, for the moment, Hamish was safe.

Hamish had spent the past fourteen frenetic hours first securing a taxi, then hopping two city busses and switching to a regional commuter train, and finally zigzagging two hundred eighty-seven tedious miles in a dirty and dented three-year-old rental car from one of those low-budget agencies situated a full two miles from the airport. Whenever possible, he kept to the secondary roads, heeded all the traffic signs, and was ever careful about seamlessly meshing with the current traffic flow. All of these were things that Hamish had never before done in his entire privileged life. He was a Tumorington, for heaven's sake! Tumoringtons do *not* take public transportation. Tumoringtons do *not* hire used, unwashed automobiles from an establishment called Cheap Heaps Are Us! For that matter, Tumoringtons do not lease cars, period. Tumoringtons have chauffeurs, servants, personal aides, housekeepers, and butlers. Tumoringtons have *people* to deal with the banal tasks of life. Tumoringtons have wealth, power, connections, and social status. Prison life, the realization hitting him as if he had just been punched in the jaw, had stripped Hamish of what he had most cherished in his heretofore über-privileged life—being a *Tumorington*.

Hamish, whatever else, was fiendishly clever. He had forced himself to travel as he had precisely because he knew no one would expect him to behave in such a plebian manner. For the moment, Hamish wore no crested navy-blue blazer, no Stefano Ricci tie, no Martin Dingman saltwater crocodile Venetians, no khakis creased sharp enough to slice prosciutto. His preferred attire, perhaps too out of place even for here, would simply have to wait. No, Hamish had secured his current wardrobe during his first—and, he fervently prayed to the stars above, last—daring venture inside the alien walls of a Walmart Supercenter earlier in the day. He now looked—well, ordinary, inconspicuous, middle class. His precise, premeditated movements constituted the very beginning steps of the detailed, complex plan that, with far too much idle time on his hands, he had painstakingly concocted and cleverly fine-tuned to the point of perfection. He was a free man at last—and nothing could or would stop him from carrying out his diabolical plan of vengeful retribution.

The escape itself, somewhat surprisingly, had been straightforward and uneventful. After Hamish had been tried for and convicted of murder—the cruel, biased media coverage and accompanying incessant public humiliation had been near unbearable—his high ten-figure bank account had been put to immediate use by a crack team of highly compensated lawyers, international business associates, well-connected political cronies, and influential family members. Within months of his incarceration, his cadre of avid supporters had been successful in getting Hamish transferred to a medium-level security facility, a place where the daily ritual of prison life, though still not tolerable for a Tumorington man by any stretch of the imagination, was not quite as horrific as the hellhole to which he had first been sent.

His loyal group of supporters had not stopped there, however. After another two years of borderline ethical manipulations, intense political wrangling, and quasi-legal machinations, during which time they had called in "overdue favors" from strategically placed local, regional, and national authorities, Hamish had been transferred yet again, this time to a federal prison camp. (A federal prison camp is, by definition, a facility that has the lowest level of security in the vast United States government penal system. The typical inmate—if there is such a thing as typical in an operation where the rampant, inherent mind-numbing bureaucracy of the United States federal government holds sway—is a person who has been caught and convicted for a nonviolent crime like embezzlement or tax evasion. Prisoners "lucky" enough to land in a federal prison camp rarely, if ever, break the rules; doing so will result in an immediate, non-appealable transfer to an institution with far stricter rules and much harsher treatment. Because of this, the staff-to-inmate ratio is low when compared to other facilities in the American penal system and the perimeter fencing is significantly more limited and less daunting; in more than a few places, surrounding walls are virtually non-existent.)

No one likes being in prison, but Hamish had despised it to the point that he thought he was going mad—Edgar Allan Poe's Roderick Usher type of mad. Even at the minimum-security facility, the confinement remained unbearable, the food vile, the guards brutish, the warden indifferent, the other inmates despicable, cliquish, deadly. More than a few had preyed upon him, sensing his frailty, naiveté, and vulnerability. Only his money and connections had kept the subhumans at bay. But how long would that last? How long could that last?

At first, Hamish had hoped that the better conditions—to his way of thinking, they were only less bad—at the minimum-security camp would allow him to eventually adjust, if only with great reluctance, to the considerable mental and physical rigors of incarceration. But he just could not do it. The temptation to escape had been too great to overcome—and eventually, it had gotten the best of him. In his new federal prison camp, it had been easy for Hamish to choose the specific time and place where, escape plan intact, he could and would simply walk away. By the time the shocked staff realized he had gone, Hamish P. Tumorington had had a two-hour head start.

Hamish knew full well that there would be hell to pay for those who had vouched for him in order that he might be successful in securing his second transfer. He had promised—no, *sworn*—that if the highly irregular transfer to a minimum-security camp were approved, he would obey *all* the prison rules. No, he had sworn to do even better than that. He would be a model prisoner for all the world to see. He would prove that even naive liberal do-gooders, like blind squirrels finding their rare acorns, could, once in a proverbial blue moon, get it right: There *are* occasions when convicted murderers, no matter how heinous their crimes, *can* obey all the rules and become fully rehabilitated. At the time, perhaps even Hamish himself had believed this tripe, but now, none of that mattered one iota. He was *free*, and he was never, ever going back.

Hamish's escape route had brought him to the quaint, off-the-beaten-path town of Mount Dora in central Florida, a place he had purposely chosen with much advance research and great care. With its current population close to twelve thousand, Mount Dora was originally settled in 1874 by restless Winter Park, Florida, natives David M. Simpson, his wife, and two children. Because the greater Orlando area, from David and his family's perspective, had been getting entirely too crowded, he and his family had eventually decided that they needed more space. The virtually empty verdant hills overlooking a pristine, shimmering lake twenty-five miles to the northwest had been their unanimous choice. *They should see the metropolitan Orlando area today!* Over the next century and a half, Mount Dora had slowly morphed into what it is today: a bustling little lakefront community well known for its funky craft and art festivals, quirky antique shops, trendy restaurants, motley flea markets, meticulously preserved historical buildings, stylish music festivals, chic promenade theater productions, amateur sailing regattas, holiday town-square–lighting festivities, ever-balmy weather, offbeat ecotourist activities, and seductive "Old Florida" charm.

Perhaps Mount Dora's most famous landmark was the Lakeside Inn, the historic landmark hotel where Hamish was now holed up. Hamish's meticulous research had indicated that he would blend in perfectly in Mount Dora and the Lakeside Inn, where diversity was the standard and eclectic the norm. Indeed, Hamish now knew that he had chosen well. No one would ever think to look for him here. No one. (The Lakeside Inn, Hamish knew, had first opened its doors in 1883, making it the oldest continuously operating business of its kind in the state of Florida. Over the years, the Lakeside Inn's stream of celebrity visitors had included, among others, Calvin Coolidge, Thomas Edison, Henry Ford, and Dwight D. Eisenhower. The inn had been successful, for a variety of serendipitous reasons, in dodging the wrecking ball in the final quarter of the twentieth century, a particularly challenging period when the hotel had faced significant cash-flow difficulties and an increasing need for significant restoration and modernization. Today, with proud new ownership, a much-needed influx of capital, and creative professional management, the storied all-wooden structure had been experiencing a heady period of revival and renaissance.)

Hamish had carefully chosen Mount Dora for another strategic reason: The town was only forty-five minutes from the Orlando International Airport. The airport's especially easy access and continuous stream of multinational, multilingual visitors would make it the perfect melting pot from which he could inconspicuously begin his forthcoming journey halfway across the globe. Hamish was going to New Zealand to find Esther.

Esther!—that vile busybody who haughtily roamed the hallowed grounds of Old Bunbury Golf & Reading Links as if she owned the place. Esther!—that incompetent and arrogant shrew who, disguised as a waitress, gave new meaning to insolent, mediocre service. Esther!—that inexplicable favorite and personal confidant of long-time Old Bunbury Club President Clive Endive Ogive IV. Esther!—that amateur sleuth whose knowledge of all things Old Bunbury was the main reason, perhaps the only reason, he had been captured and convicted. Esther!—that insufferable harridan who would now pay, and pay dearly, for all the misery she had caused him.

Yes, Hamish knew full well that Esther was currently in New Zealand. His many well-compensated informants kept meticulous track of the evil wench's every movement. For some inexplicable reason, Hamish knew, Esther was fascinated with all things New Zealand and that she had been "rewarded" by the Old Bunbury Board of Directors for her part in his capture and conviction. *REWARDED! How vile and ironic!* Had he wanted, Hamish could have had Esther's earthly existence terminated at the time and place of his choosing by an anonymous professional—someone who could have easily made her welcome demise look like an accident. No one ever need know the truth. Perhaps it would be misconstrued as a doddering, elderly lady's tragic loss of balance and subsequent fall to her mortal demise from one of New Zealand's myriad low-fenced remote scenic outlooks. Perhaps it might be seen as an unfortunate fatal auto accident because a faltering, foolish crone had inexplicably lost control on one of New Zealand's tortuously narrow winding roads. No, Hamish would do the dirty deed himself in the place and circumstances of his own choosing. It was all part of his cunning master plan. Sweet, sweet revenge would belong to Hamish—and Hamish alone.

With a broad, wickedly satisfying grin now spanning his face, Hamish collapsed atop the room's antique four-poster bed. In less than a minute, and for the first time since the fateful day of his arrest, Hamish fell into a deep, peaceful, dreamless sleep.

Mount Dora's main intersection—Donnelly Street and 5th Avenue—as it looked in 1926.

Chapter 12

The Pancake Rocks and Franz Josef Glacier

Esther's night at the stylish Coleraine Motel was, as it turned out, a quiet, restful one. She had been able, in relatively short order, to put the disconcerting news of Hamish's unanticipated prison escape completely out of her mind. If need be, Esther could be singularly focused and devastatingly logical—though she much preferred whimsy and serendipity as her life's core guiding principles—and she had been quick to calculate that the odds were low that Hamish would seek her out here in New Zealand. Even if he did, his getting to New Zealand and pinpointing her exact location were highly problematic; it would be like finding the proverbial needle in a haystack. No, she was safe for now. Back in the United States, it might be a different matter, but she could and would deal with that at the appropriate time. Perhaps President Clive was right about Hamish likely being apprehended before she once again set foot on United States soil, but Esther had a bad feeling on that count. Hamish, Esther knew all too well from her decades at Old Bunbury, was enormously wealthy, extremely well connected, fiendishly clever, and, most importantly, doggedly determined. Like people of means and members of private clubs everywhere, Hamish was not a happy camper when things didn't go *exactly* the way he thought they should. Yes, she would have to be careful.

But enough of this. Fretting about what might happen was, Esther knew better than a Japanese Zen master who had attained true enlightenment, a monumental waste of one's precious time here on good planet Earth. No, better to live in the moment and continue on with her general plan to explore and enjoy the South Island's spectacularly beautiful west coast as she meandered her way down towards Queenstown.

Following a quick stop for a large caramel mocha latté at the McDonald's in the heart of Greymouth—while Esther didn't particularly care for all of McDonald's offerings, she always thought the company did a consistently credible job with their new McCafés—Esther headed north on Route 6 towards her first destination of the day: the Pancake Rocks.

The Pancake Rocks, located in Paparoa National Park at tiny Dolomite Point near the little coastal settlement of Punakaiki, was one of Esther's very favorite natural attractions in all of New Zealand—and that was saying something. Looking eerily like multistory stacks of giant buckwheat pancakes, these curious rock formations had first formed about thirty million years ago more than a mile beneath the raging sea. Over tens of thousands of years, alternating layers of sand and assorted dead and decaying marine creatures had become buried and compressed on the ocean floor. Eventually, the immense pressure of the water, in conjunction with the laws of chemistry, had caused these multiple layers of organic and inorganic matter to solidify into hard limestone and softer sandstone. Then, not all that long ago (geologically speaking), intense seismic action had spasmodically lifted the strange formations above the seabed, and the ongoing combination of mildly acidic rain, stiff ocean winds, and ever-present saline water had combined to erode the sandstone more quickly than the limestone, thereby carving out the bizarre pancake shapes that awestruck visitors gaze at today.

The official New Zealand parks and recreation website, when describing the Pancake Rocks area, says that it is an easy "twenty-minute loop" to see the rock formations and nearby coastal cliffs, blowholes, and surge pools; it took Esther nearly an hour and a half. This was her third visit, yet she still found the sights along the stepping stone walkway and trodden-earthen path mesmerizing to the point that she had to remind herself on several occasions to stop gawking and keep moving. Plus, Lady Luck was with her this fine morning; it was high tide. At that time, the ocean swells are sufficiently elevated to rush headlong through the narrow vertical limestone shafts dotting the beachfront and impel sizeable potent combinations of water and compressed air upward. The results are breathtaking: rhythmic, geyser-like plumes of hissing, foaming, spraying saltwater, with majestic bursts occasionally reaching as high as seventy-five feet.

As she was pulling out of the parking lot, her acute New Zealand wanderlust and ever-present intellectual curiosity temporarily quenched, Esther calculated that, even allowing for several stops along the way to savor the breathtaking coastal views as well as to take in a leisurely lunch, she could easily make the one-hundred-and-ten–mile drive south on Route 6 and be at the remote little service village of Franz Josef, about three miles from the face of the acclaimed glacier of the same name, no later than one thirty. This would give her more than enough time to book the highly touted afternoon Glacier Valley Walk—something that she had often read about but had never done—find a nice place to stay, have dinner, and settle in for the night. (Esther already knew that the first European descriptions of the glacier had been made by awestruck passengers aboard the deck of the globetrotting steamship *Mary Louisa* in 1859. In 1865, the glacier had been formally christened after Emperor Franz Josef I of Austria by the German explorer Julius von Haast. Interestingly enough, Esther also remembered that the glacier has been *advancing* (to the acute consternation of pseudo-intellectual, man-made–global-warming, agenda-driven dorks around the globe) a little over two *feet* per day since 1984, a lightning-like speed by glacial standards. Her recollection of these most interesting data made Esther all the more eager to thoroughly explore her next major destination.

The Glacier Valley Walk, as it turned out, was even better than she had imagined. The route began with an easy stroll through the heavily wooded, verdant path along the mighty Waiho, the river emerging from the terminus of the glacier. After a relatively short and mild climb, Esther was rewarded with an expansive, unblocked view of the famous Franz Josef

Glacier itself. Immobilized by the glacier's massive size and shimmering beauty, Esther sat, stared, and mentally photographed the intricate details of the ponderous chunk of jagged bluish-white ice framed against the crystal-clear cerulean backdrop for over an hour, intent upon indelibly imprinting the glacier's spectacular beauty onto her permanent memory banks. Finally, she stood, smiled, and made the gradual downhill lope back to her Camry. It was, she knew, time to secure her night's lodgings.

Esther's choices were limited in a village so tiny, so, after a brief review of the available options, she decided on the High Peaks Hotel, primarily because of its unobstructed views of both Mount Cook ("Aoraki" in the native Maori tongue, and the highest peak in all of New Zealand) and nearby Mount Tasman. It turned out to be an excellent choice. The vista of the two snowcapped peaks from the hotel was indeed dramatic, and the room that the friendly and accommodating owners, Marlene and Alan Chant, showed her was warm, clean, inviting, comfortable, and reasonably priced. Yes, this quaint little out-of-the-way hotel would do just fine for tonight's stopover.

Esther decided to have her evening repast right at the hotel's restaurant; she was pleasantly tired from another day of intense touring and saw no need to drive back into town. Marlene, who also served as the restaurant's chef and chief bottle washer, graciously welcomed Esther to her prime window table, handed her a menu, and promptly suggested the herb-crusted rack of lamb, the specialty of the house.

Esther was not disappointed. The meal was expertly prepared, artfully presented, and professionally served. Esther even treated herself to a glass of 2009 Corbans Cottage Block Hawke's Bay Chardonnay, voted in 2012 one of New Zealand's finest by a distinguished panel of oenologists.

"Thank you so much for a wonderful dinner, Marlene," Esther said, standing beside her table as she was preparing to return to her room. "Everything was absolute perfect. This is my first time here at your lovely hotel, but I will surely return on my next visit to the South Island. I also will be sure to tell all my stateside friends about your charming little hotel and restaurant."

"You are most welcome, Esther. It was truly our pleasure meeting and chatting with you. Alan and I think you are one *very* adventurous young lady. I dare say you've been to many more place in New Zealand than most all of us natives. Very impressive, indeed! We look forward to seeing you again and hope you enjoy the rest of your stay here in our beautiful and unspoiled country."

"That I will, Marlene. That I will."

Fifteen minutes later, Esther was snuggled into her cozy warm bed and already half asleep, another whirlwind day of touring her beloved New Zealand swirling in her head. *Life is good.*

Paparoa National Park's curious Pancake Rocks overlook is one of Esther's favorite natural attractions in all of New Zealand, if not the entire world.

Chapter 13

Hamish on the Move

Consciousness returned to Hamish with the speed of a sore-footed butterfly touching ground. For several minutes, the sheer sensual pleasure and accompanying mental well-being that had washed over him—the direct result, no doubt, of his first uninterrupted, deep, and dreamless sleep since the fateful day of his nightmarish arrest—prevented Hamish from fully realizing, and, more to the point, even caring about realizing, exactly who and where he was. When his near-sybaritic recumbent euphoria had sufficiently dissipated, reality hit him like a cold slap across the face and he bolted erect in the blanket-strewn bed. The frightening, threatening details of his present situation came flooding back. Hamish was in his second-floor room at the Lakeside Inn in Mount Dora, Florida; he had just escaped from prison and was on the run from the police. Obviously, because no one had accosted him during his first glorious night as a free man, Hamish had remained successful in his vigilant efforts to elude his many determined pursuers.

His considerable deductive powers now fully functioning, Hamish reveled in the delicious fact that with each passing hour, the odds of his being captured significantly diminished—a thought that brought more than a hint of sinister smile to his unshaven face. No, nothing would deter him from executing the next steps of his cunning master plan of well-justified revenge and retribution.

For the first time since he had checked in late the previous evening, Hamish took a close, measured look around his generously sized room. A good portion of the furnishings and fixtures, he rued, were tired to the point of needing of either significant restoration or outright replacement. However,

Hamish's highly attuned sense of decor and decorum also told him that his room and accoutrements had once been elegant, stylish, desirable. After a bit, he focused on the sack-back Windsor armchair in the far corner of the room—it was an imitation, Hamish knew only too well, although one of good-quality materials and steady-handed workmanship—covered with two faux Victorian-era pillows.

Ah, pillows. Hamish had once been internationally revered as a true aficionado in the rarified air of private-club pillow selection, maintenance, repair, and replacement. Whatever else people might now be saying about him, they could not question the fact that Hamish remained as talented in and knowledgeable about the intricacies and nuances of the heady world of private-club pillows as anyone alive. It was not all that long ago when Hamish had, in fact, emerged as one of two finalists to break the seemingly insurmountable gender barrier on the Old Bunbury Golf Links & Reading Club's Pillow Committee—to his way of thinking, *the* most coveted committee assignment in the entire world of private clubs. Ironically, Hamish had been about to be appointed to the prestigious position, something that would have been the crowning achievement to his already impressive resume of private-club committee assignments, but the offer had never materialized. Instead, he had been summarily arrested for making that low-life, womanizing, gambling-addicted nebbish Alfie Johnson pay the ultimate price for his pathetic life—ironically, a life that was clearly incongruous with membership in a club as exclusive and esteemed as Old Bunbury.

Ah, private-club pillow committees, Hamish continued to obsess, unable for the moment to leave a topic so near and dear to his heart. Unlike most private-club committees, which are typically focused on one specific task or a single area of operation, pillow committees are unique in that they have multiple core responsibilities, all of which are fundamental to the very existence of private clubs as the free world has come to know and cherish them. Pillow committees, to begin with, must ensure that all the pillows throughout the entirety of the clubhouse are properly fluffed and perfectly situated at all times; they also must meticulously coordinate the appropriate ongoing repair and/or replacement of pillows as (sadly) they become worn or, heaven forbid, frayed; in addition, pillow committee members are ever-vigilant in their Herculean efforts to guarantee that all areas of a private club truly in need of pillows not only have them but also have the appropriate style, size, shape, and, if necessary, tasseling; and, lastly but certainly not least, private-club pillow committees are ever attentive to the heady issue—one that may have serious repercussions for a private club's long-term financial and social viability—of objectively evaluating the myriad pros and cons of "re-covering versus purchasing new." It was no wonder every *thinking* private club member's ultimate ambition in life was to be selected to join such a prestigious and versatile group.

But enough! Any more of this painful reminiscing and he would drive himself totally mad—something that, he realized, prison life may very well have already done to him. *WAS he mad?*

Hamish forced himself to refocus on the task at hand. He knew that he had to be at the Orlando International Airport in little more than three hours, from whence he would begin the long and arduous journey to New Zealand. He would, for the first time in his highly sheltered and über-privileged life, be flying coach. *Coach!* Hamish shuddered at the very absurdity of the thought. *How utterly obscene! The vile things one must do to minimize the chances of being recognized and getting caught.* No, he should not remain alone in his room, overpowered by such sordid thoughts—far better to keep occupied. Accordingly, with a couple of hours to kill, Hamish chose to wash, shave, dress, pack, check out of his room, and find an appropriate place in downtown Mount Dora in which to enjoy an inconspicuous and leisurely lunch.

Quite by accident, Hamish stumbled upon Cody's on 4th. As it turned out, his afternoon repast was one of the very best culinary experiences of his entire life—and for someone as well-traveled and gastronomically astute as Hamish, that was saying a mouthful. The quaint little café, tastefully decorated to recall and celebrate the special charm and rich history of Mount Dora, featured aromatic coffees, delectable pastries, freshly prepared salads, innovative sandwiches, homemade soups, savory quiches, and an excellent selection of domestic and foreign beers and wines, all professionally served by a knowledgeable, warm, and caring staff. No wonder the place had earned four and a half stars on Trip Advisor! To Hamish's way of thinking, it was one of the very few culinary establishments in the entire world that should garner a perfect five-star rating; anything less must obviously be driven by nothing more than sheer ignorance or mean-spirited, irrational personal agenda.

After reviewing the blackboard detailing the various specials of the day—Cody herself had graciously taken the time to describe the menu to him in mouth-watering detail—Hamish mindfully placed his order. His first course was a cup of Cody's unique "kale verde soup," a heavenly chicken-based concoction whose major ingredients included fresh curly-leaved kale, spicy Italian sausage, parboiled new potatoes, shredded baby carrots, and assorted herbs and spices. Hamish's entree of choice was a generous wedge of Cody's freshly baked crustless "farmer's quiche," a "Cody-original" custard of eggs, milk, and cream enhanced (filled) with crisply sautéed bacon, shredded cheddar, parmesan, mozzarella, julienned green and red peppers, and baby broccoli florets. He finished off his delightful meal with a thick slice of Cody's scrumptious homemade carrot cake, a treat so divine and internationally famous that it now motivated patrons from four continents to make annual pilgrimages to Mount Dora. The lunch, in fact, was so delicious that, had he not had his other pressing business, Hamish would surely have added another day or two to his stay at the Lakeside Inn just so he could sample a broader selection of the five-star fare of Cody's on 4th. But, alas, Hamish's plans called for him to press on.

Paying in cash and leaving a generous tip—but not *too* generous, as he did not want to be remembered as anything more than yet another giddily satisfied patron—Hamish made it a point to thank Cody personally on his way out of her fantastic little dining establishment, vowing to himself that he would return, and return often, once his "work" with Esther had been completed.

The moderate midafternoon traffic flow allowed Hamish to complete the drive to Orlando International Airport in forty-seven minutes. After leaving his car in the long-term lot and checking in at the airline's main counter, Hamish slowly made his way towards the lengthy security lines on the B side of the terminal. Doing his best to blend in inconspicuously with those waiting in the Occasional Travelers queue, a twinge of doubt, not dissimilar to a mild electric current, shot through his temporarily addled brain. *Will my new documents pass muster?* Yes, he immediately reassured himself; he had paid top dollar for the complete new identity that his powerful and well-connected friends had painstakingly, secretly assembled and stashed for him in a safe deposit box along yesterday's route. Hamish, in fact, now had in his possession all the necessities for verifying his new, unblemished self: a United States passport; a Florida drivers license; an American Express gold card; a Bank of America Visa card; a Lake County, Florida, library card; and other assorted ancillary documents all confirming that the man holding them was one Rich V. Steele.

Indeed, Mr. Steele made it through the Transportation Security Administration screening process without incident; no one gave the rather ordinary-looking middle-aged man in the shoddily made off-the-rack workingman's clothes so much as a second look. Thirty-five minutes later, he was boarding, along with his fellow Zone 2 passengers, the first of three jets that would transport him to Christchurch, New Zealand.

Even though Hamish P. Tumorington was fortunate enough to have dined in hundreds of the world's very finest restaurants, his expert palate told him that none were better than Mount Dora's fabulous Cody's on 4th.

Chapter 14

Onward and Downward

Esther would end up arriving in Queenstown on Wednesday around eleven in the morning, about twenty hours later than her first ad-hoc itinerary had called for. She got her usual early start on Tuesday, leaving the quaint, wonderfully accommodating High Peaks Hotel a little before seven. Esther rightly calculated that, even accounting for the unexpected and unplanned stops that she would surely make along the beautiful drive south—parts of Route 6 hugged the spectacular coastline of the Tasman Sea, she knew, while other sections wove through breathtaking mountain passes and verdant, people-empty, sheep-filled valleys—she could easily make the two-hundred-twenty-mile drive to Queenstown by midafternoon, her accustomed time to stop and secure suitable lodgings for the night. As it happened, things didn't work out that way at all. "But no matter," Esther said to no one in particular after she had suitably amended the morning's original plan. That was the beauty, Esther well knew, of having the time, temperament, and desire to be flexible.

When Esther pulled into the charming little town of Wanaka shortly before noon, she decided, on the spur of the moment, that it would be a very nice place in which to spend the remainder of the day. Wanaka was only about forty miles northeast of Queenstown if one took the ever-twisting, vista-laden Cardrona Valley Road "shortcut," surely one of the prettiest and most exhilarating drives in the entire country. But she would now postpone that particular adventure until tomorrow morning. Perhaps the past several days of steady travel and intense sightseeing had combined to take their toll. Or perhaps it was finally time to make amends for the fact that, on her previous visits to the South Island, Esther had, for reasons long forgotten, bypassed this bustling little city in the Upper Clutha River Valley. *Whatever,* she thought. It was time to stop and smell the Wanaka roses.

By the time she found a parking space, Esther had already begun to solidify her revised plan for the remainder of the day. She would have a simple lunch somewhere in downtown Wanaka, enjoy a leisurely stroll along the tree-lined lakefront promenade, and perhaps, time permitting, take in a local attraction. By then, she would be more than ready to find a nice place to settle in for the night. The afternoon would also be a good opportunity for Esther to purchase a few souvenir gifts for people back at Old Bunbury. President Clive, for example, surely deserved something extra special for flying halfway around the world to attend last Saturday's wonderful celebration at the Kaikoura Whaling & Sailing Club. And then there was Jay Morris, Old Bunbury's fine club manager. He was surely the best she had ever worked for during her lengthy tenure at the club—and she had outlasted more than a dozen. A couple of them, she now remembered, had been blatant incompetents, lazy buffoons, pernicious liars, and/or outright thieves. *No doubt Democrats.* Yes, Jay was far from perfect—he occasionally pestered her about trivial things, such as confirming her exact age and adhering to the posted work schedule—but he did have a good heart and an uncompromising work ethic, and the members, by and large, liked and respected him. And she couldn't forget Chef Henri DuBois, Old Bunbury's talented and caring chef who, for a brief period, had actually been a prime suspect in the gruesome murder of Alfie Johnson—that is, until Esther's clever undercover work and considerable powers of deductive reasoning had quickly exonerated him. Feeling especially generous, Esther thought that she might even spring for a small gift for Poinsettia Derswoggle, the dedicated but proficient-to-the-point-of-annoying waitress whose twenty-seven–year tenure at the club was second (but by a long shot) only to Esther's. All of these people, no matter their foibles, were *very* important to Esther; they were an integral part of the Old Bunbury family, of which she was unwaveringly proud to belong. They, along with the other members and remaining staff, in combination with the club's long and storied history, unique customs, and rich traditions, were what made Old Bunbury so special.

Wanaka, Esther now remembered, had originally been settled by few particularly adventurous Europeans during New Zealand's manic gold rush of the mid-nineteenth century. Today, the town, situated at the extreme southern end of the pristine waters of Lake Wanaka, has about ten thousand permanent residents and is primarily a resort town featuring both summer and winter seasons. More and more New Zealanders actually prefer it to Queenstown because, at least for the time being, it remains considerably less commercialized, and perhaps also because it is one of the few areas in the entire country to enjoy a truly continental climate, offering its citizens four distinct seasons.

Following a thoroughly satisfying lunch at the Kai Whakapai Cafe and Bar—every once in a while, Esther just *had* to return to the culinary basics with a charbroiled hamburger on a toasted white-bread bun (smothered, of course, in onions, lettuce, pickles, and ketchup) complemented by thick-cut French fries and a real Coke—Esther spent the next two hours strolling Ardmore Street and savoring its jaw-dropping views of Lake Wanaka and the surrounding snow-laden mountain peaks. She could see why the early European settlers had stayed after the frenzy of the gold-rush era had run its course. Esther also popped into a couple of eclectic boutiques along the way and was successful in her quest to purchase several souvenir gifts.

Esther, ever the offbeat adventurer, decided next to visit Stuart Landsborough's Puzzling World, a unique forty-five-year-old attraction about which she had previously read very favorable reviews in several of her New Zealand guidebooks as well as online. She thoroughly enjoyed her hour wandering the giant labyrinth, viewing the assorted holograms, and visiting the various optical-illusion rooms. Esther thought Puzzling World was a place that children from all around the world, no matter their wealth, ancestry, nationality or education, would find especially entertaining.

By the time Esther checked in to her spacious studio apartment at the Clearbrook Motel, a conveniently located, well-appointed facility in the center of town, it was close to five o'clock. Bernice Innes, who, along with her husband, Dougal, owned and operated the property, welcomed her with open arms.

"Thank you for choosing our motel, Esther. It is so nice to meet you," Bernice said graciously.

"And you as well. I was wondering if you might do me a favor, Bernice. My hectic pace of travel over the past several days has, I regret to admit, finally caught up with me. I would like to have a pizza delivered to my room, sit on my balcony and enjoy the wonderful views, catch up on some laundry and e-mails, watch a little television, and retire early. Tomorrow, I may even sleep in before I make the short drive down to Queenstown. Do you know a place nearby that makes good pizza and will deliver?" she asked.

"I certainly do, Esther. Tell you what—you let me know what specific toppings you prefer, and I will take care of everything. So now why don't you just head over to your room and relax?"

"Thank you, Bernice. How very kind of you."

And that is exactly what Esther did—with one addition. Esther thought it was high time to send a travel-update text to President Clive, so she carefully thumb-typed the following: "Hello, boss. Thank you again for taking the time to come to New Zealand for my dinner at the Kaikoura Whaling & Sailing Club. It was one of the very best surprises of my long and blessed life! I am now in the beautiful little resort town of Wanaka. Tomorrow morning, I will be making the short drive south to Queenstown, where I plan to settle in for a few days. You are probably on your flight home even as I compose this message. When you get back, please give my very best to everyone at Old Bunbury. I look forward to seeing you late next week at the club."

Fifteen minutes later, Esther was fast asleep.

Esther thoroughly enjoyed her visit to the beautiful little South Island resort town of Wanaka.

Chapter 15

Down Under

Handing his opened United States passport and hastily completed royal-blue New Zealand passenger arrival card to the nattily dressed customs officer—one Franklin Panapa—Mr. Steele proffered a deferential, unassuming good-morning. Hamish did not have to feign either exhaustion or untidiness for the seemingly disinterested agent. To the contrary, Hamish found it unfathomable that *anyone* could travel in coach, let alone survive a marathon trans-Pacific crossing, without arriving a sleep-deprived, sartorially disheveled wreck. Hamish certainly *looked* the part of the ordinary, happy-to-have-finally-arrived but road-weary traveler.

"Is this your first visit to New Zealand, Mr. Steele?" Franklin Panapa asked with a mechanical roteness that made the typical Catholic recitation of the rosary seem like an intensely focused exercise in Maslow's self-actualization. At the same time and in a not dissimilar manner, Mr. Panapa deftly swiped Mr. Steele's passport through the electronic scanner affixed to his computer screen.

"Yes, sir," Hamish answered, doing his best to strike the appropriate balance between politeness and respect.

"I see that you have not indicated the main reason for your visit. Business? Pleasure?" queried the weary agent.

"I'm very sorry, sir," said Hamish near obsequiously, his addled brain unwittingly flashing to the sybaritic joy that would surely permeate his entire being once he had successfully completed his "business" with Esther. "I'm a professional travel blogger, but writing about your beautiful country will surely feel like a vacation to me," Hamish continued sheepishly. "I just couldn't decide between business and holiday/vacation. You are indeed correct in that I should have checked the appropriate category. My sincerest apologies. Business it is," said Hamish, retrieving the form and making the appropriate change.

"Business," repeated Mr. Panapa, pleased that both the passenger arrival card was now correctly completed and that Mr. Steele's swiped passport had just passed muster. Franklin Panapa *hated* irregularities. *Americans always seem to have more trouble than most with routine rules and procedures. Maybe it's something in their water.* Then again, they were surely the only populace in the entire world dumb and naive enough to elect, and then *re-elect,* someone like Obama to their nation's highest office.

"If only everyone loved their work as much as you obviously do," Mr. Panapa rued, a noble attempt to prove that even people who work in desultory, mind-numbing jobs can, when the situation requires, be pleasantly conversant. "Have a wonderful stay in New Zealand, Mr. Steele," he threw in for good measure. Franklin Panapa's old-fashioned customs stamp kerchunked its unique mark onto Hamish's otherwise virgin passport, an act that irrevocably confirmed he had now finished with this particular visitor and had already turned his attention to the next person in the long, seemingly never-ending line.

Hamish would have to be more careful in the future. *Whatever you do, do* not *call attention to yourself. Your failure to fill out the customs form correctly was both careless and foolish.* No, he knew deep inside, it was more than that; it was his deliberate and petulant little way of snubbing his nose at the maddeningly idiotic, unchecked bureaucracy that apparently now spanned the entire globe. *Your American accent and apparent "attitude" already make you stand out from the madding crowd. THINK!*

Hamish, like freedom-loving, self-respecting people the world over, utterly despised big government and all the blatant waste, intrusive interference into the lives of citizenry, and bizarre gobbledygook it entailed. While Hamish differed substantially from the Old Bunbury crowd in many and substantial ways, his abhorrence of all that Obama and his nefarious, bald-face lying, condescending, Constitution-attacking cronies were continuing to foist on the unwitting American populace remained one thing that they, together with all clear-thinking people around the globe, would always have in common.

"Rich V. Steele," Hamish mouthed to no one in particular. He loved the way the three little innocuous syllables so naturally rolled off his tongue. It certainly was not a name that Hamish had chosen at random. No, it was a carefully chosen moniker reflecting Hamish's fiendishly clever mind and warped sense of humor. Perhaps, in some dark Freudian manner, it was also his haughty way of dropping a few tantalizing intellectual breadcrumbs for those foolish enough to think they could actually find and stop him.

The first name, Rich, was plain enough in and of itself—the kind of name that people quickly forget because of its very ordinariness—but to Hamish, it was more; it was a perversely satisfying opportunity for savoring the special irony of having a new first name that so well matched his lofty financial status.

The middle initial—V—aptly mirrored the P in his real name. On the surface, the two letters, one aspirated and the other not, were nothing more than a harmless pair of rhyming consonants, but to Hamish, the similarity went deeper. While the P in Hamish's name stood for Pictorious, his long-deceased mother's maiden name—a surname, he was proud to note, whose history-laden origins dated back to the Quran, the Bible, and the Bhagavadgītā—he saw the V as the perfect rhyming omen for his emerging *victorious* over Esther, Clive, and all things Old Bunbury.

Steele was, again, a common enough American-sounding name, one that would certainly not attract undue attention, but, to Hamish, a word synonymous with insurmountable strength and dogged determination, a term most appropriate in confirming his unwavering resolve for his forthcoming cathartic retribution. *Yes, you have chosen well, Rich V. Steele.*

Hamish retrieved his luggage and secured his rental car without incident. As he was carefully making his way out of the airport's confusing parking lot—it had been quite a while since Hamish had last driven on the left-hand side of the road—he knew it was time to turn on his untraceable prepaid cellular phone. It took less than a minute for Telecom New Zealand to pinpoint his new position and reset his phone to the correct local time zone. That process successfully completed, Hamish was ready to place the prearranged call. After pulling over to the side of the road—the *last* thing Hamish needed was a traffic ticket—he carefully punched the United States exit code (011), the New Zealand country code (64), and the telephone number he knew by heart.

"Yes," whispered a neutral, nondescript voice on the other end of the line.

"This is Rich V. Steele," said Hamish, doing his best to mask the tone and timbre of his natural voice pattern.

"Mr. Steele, may I have your confirmation code, please?" queried a guarded voice.

Upon hearing the correct recitation of the previously agreed-upon random combination of letters and numbers, the person on the other end said, "Mr. Steele, I want to let you know that Queenstown is especially beautiful this time of year. I suggest you consider paying that beautiful city a visit." With that, the line abruptly went dead.

His people had done their work well. *Esther was in or heading to Queenstown!* Their efforts to trace and monitor Esther's texts from New Zealand had obviously proven successful.

As he programmed "Queenstown, Otago, New Zealand" into his car's third-generation global positioning system, Hamish made no attempt to repress the sinister smile that was rapidly spreading across his still-handsome face.

Although Rich V. Steele had quite sinister things on his mind, he couldn't help appreciating the spectacular natural beauty of New Zealand's South Island.

Chapter 16

A Surprise Confrontation

Queenstown, for a variety of synergistic reasons, had always ranked near the top of Esther's short list of preferred New Zealand destinations—and she is not alone in her considered opinion. This sophisticated, cosmopolitan resort in the western Otago region of the South Island, a place with less than twenty-five thousand permanent residents, manages to attract and entertain close to two million visitors a year. People from scores of nations spanning the globe "flock" to, and thoroughly delight in, all that this vibrant little city has to offer. *Perhaps it has something to do with the untold millions of sheep that are gradually, maybe even surreptitiously, overtaking this beautiful part of the world.*

Esther had been to Queenstown on three previous occasions, yet the nonstop, pulsating energy and unmistakable cachet of the internationally known mini-metropolis, in combination with the encircling Alpine peaks and shimmering waters of Lake Wakatipu, never ceased to refocus, revitalize, and reenergize her. Driving into what more than a few North Americans have wistfully nicknamed the Vail of the southern hemisphere on this glorious Wednesday morning, Esther was confident that her fourth visit would be no different.

Esther's schedule for the day broke her usual mold. The very first item on her still-fluid agenda would be securing a lake-facing room, hopefully one with a private balcony, at the modern Tanoa Aspen Hotel, a beautiful oasis boasting the highest lodging elevation in the entire city. Even though it was currently the off season, Esther didn't want to take any chances that one of her preferred rooms might not be available. She had stayed at this well-appointed, customer-service–driven facility on past visits and believed that, all things considered, the

Tanoa Aspen offered unbeatable views of both Lake Wakatipu and The Remarkables, the snowcapped, saw-toothed mountain range rising abruptly along the southeastern shore of Queenstown's own fifty-mile-long, twelve-hundred-feet-deep crystal-clear body of water.

(For as long as she could remember, Esther had, in fact, been fascinated by the dueling explanations as to how The Remarkables had garnered their name. The officially sanctioned version, Esther knew, was that one Alexander Garvie had christened the mountains The Remarkables in 1858 because they are apparently one of only two mountain ranges on the entire planet that align directly perpendicular to the equator. *Who would know, or actually care about knowing, such an arcane fact, especially in the middle of the nineteenth century?* Esther, however, found such a "purely academic" accounting neither compelling nor even particularly credible. She much preferred the second—and clearly more romantic and fanciful—explanation: Early Queenstown settlers, upon gazing at the beautiful mountains one glorious winter evening, with the sun near-blinding in its potent reflection off the snowcapped peaks, exclaimed in rapturous unison that the massive jagged peaks directly across the lake were truly remarkable to behold.)

Esther spent the first two hours after checking in—yes, she was lucky enough to secure a room that met her specifications—simply sitting on her balcony and letting her eyes drink in The Remarkables' awe-inspiring views. Nature in all its splendor was on full display, and Esther was content—no, she was more than that; she was truly at peace with who she was and the beautiful world in which she felt truly blessed to reside—to just sit and stare. Like she did at so many other spectacularly beautiful sites around New Zealand, Esther strove mightily to indelibly imprint—as far as it was humanly possible—as many details of the panoramic view now in front of her onto her permanent memory banks.

Hunger finally getting the best of her, Esther opted to make the short drive into town and enjoy a late lunch. Ideally, she would savor a meal substantial enough that, when she returned to the hotel, a light snack by the roaring fire of the Panorama Bar—most likely complemented with a glass or two of one of her favorite South Island Chardonnays—would be all the sustenance she would require before turning in for the evening.

Following a well-prepared, cordially served specialty of the house at the Pig & Whistle, the traditional English-style pub located in the heart of town—this time, her third visit, she had their famous Richmond roast, a hearty helping of Southland slow-roasted prime beef served with roasted Irish potatoes, sugar snap peas, thick homemade gravy, and Yorkshire pudding—Esther made the short walk up to the base of Skyline Gondola, the city's world-famous cable car. Opened in 1967, this engineering marvel, the steepest mountain lift in the southern hemisphere, transports tens of thousands of giddy riders each year a half mile upwards toward to the summit of Bob's Peak. Esther had made and enjoyed the dramatic ascent on all three of her previous visits to Queenstown, and this time would be no different. The outdoor cantilevered viewing platform, nearly a third of a mile above the city center, offered a two-hundred-twenty–degree panoramic view of Coronet Peak, Walter Peak, Cecil Peak, Lake Wakatipu, The Remarkables, and the thriving Queenstown metropolis.

As Esther stood savoring the spectacular views, it occurred to her that this would be an excellent opportunity to respond to the text she had received from President Clive earlier in the day. He had reported that he had safely returned home to the United States, that the members and employees at Old Bunbury missed her, and that she should enjoy the rest of her stay in New Zealand. She could, she thought, greatly embellish her response by attaching a nice picture taken from the viewing platform upon which she now was standing. Even though it was just after midnight back home, Esther knew the long-time Old Bunbury president well enough to know that his cell would, in all probability, be switched to silent for the night. She could therefore compose and send her text and accompanying picture now, and Clive could and would then view her correspondence when he woke up in six or so hours and enjoyed his never-varying breakfast (a hearty bowl of Grape-Nuts topped with fresh berries and skim milk). Accordingly, Esther texted these words to go along with the excellent photo her iPhone 5 had so artfully captured: "Hello, boss. Thank you for your good text of about eight hours ago. I am happy to hear that you have now safely returned home. I am currently standing atop the viewing platform reached by the fabulous Queenstown Skyline Gondola, enjoying the awe-inspiring views of The Remarkables, Lake Wakatipu, and the cityscape below and thought you would enjoy the attached picture. I will probably stay here for another hour or so and then head back to my hotel for the evening. Please say hello to everyone at Old Bunbury for me. I look forward to seeing you next week at the club."

Fifty-five minutes later, Esther, totally at peace with herself and the extraordinarily beautiful part of the world she was currently experiencing, boarded the spacious cable car for its nine-minute descent to the docking station near the base of the mountain. She quickly exited the chalet-style headquarters building and began the short walk back to the town center. Glancing at her phone for the time, she saw that she would retrieve her car and complete the short drive back to the Tanoa Aspen Hotel before five thirty. The downtown area had, Esther noticed, become quite crowded and noisy since her ascent nearly two hours before, the sidewalks now echoing the cacophony of happy, garrulous multilingual pedestrians and the streets filled with all makes and models of zooming, ski-racked, grit-covered vehicles.

Patiently waiting with about twenty-five others for the streetlight to change, Esther felt a gentle tap on her back.

"Hello, Esther," said a quiet, familiar voice, one that she had not heard for several years. Turning, Esther found herself staring at the haggard face of Hamish P. Tumorington. His Machiavellian smile sent an uncontrollable primeval chill slithering down the length of her spine. Surprisingly, the first rational thought that entered Esther's mind had nothing to do with her personal safety; rather, it was that Hamish's time in prison had aged him well beyond his chronological years. For a brief moment, she almost felt sorry for the desperate fugitive from the law.

"Mr. Tumorington!" she gasped, too stunned to utter anything more.

"Yes, Esther, it is I, Hamish P. Tumorington. I just wanted to confirm for you in the flesh what I know you already know. I have indeed escaped from prison and have made the long incognito trek to New Zealand for one reason and one reason only—to personally deliver this message to you: One of these days, you will pay the ultimate price for what you, Clive, and Detective Giztips have done to me. I find it especially gratifying that you will never know when, where, how, or in what manner this rightful retribution will occur. The one thing I can assure you of is this: It will happen on United States soil. Accordingly, I urge you to go ahead and enjoy the rest of your stay here in New Zealand. You are, I must admit, correct about one thing: This country does indeed give new meaning to the phrase 'natural beauty.' I wish you safe travels back to the United States. It is now time for this gentleman on the lam to steal away, but I am quite certain that our paths will soon cross again."

With that, Hamish turned and quickly walked away; within seconds, he had melted into the bustling crowd.

Esther captured this spectacular panoramic view of Queenstown, The Remarkables and Lake Wakatipu on a recent visit.

Chapter 17

More than Texting

Shaking out the final few particularly stubborn droplets, Clive tried hard to remember the last time he had survived an entire night without making at least one irksome pit stop. *Ugh!* Save for those increasingly rare alcohol-induced stupors potent enough to keep consciousness at bay a full eight hours, he could not. *This senior-citizen thing surely isn't all it's cracked up to be.*

Just as he was about to collapse back into his authentic 1910 Edwardian burr walnut double bed, Clive heard his Blackberry's unique, unmistakable Dew-DOOP! "boldly" informing him a text message had just arrived. *Damn. Must have forgotten to put the thing on silent before going to bed.*

Clive proudly counted himself among the rapidly diminishing number of people in the United States who still clung loyally to their Blackberries. *Like the millions of great Americans who truly understand that Obama is an America-hating, narcissistic socialist supposedly cling to their religion and guns?* He knew full well that fewer than ten percent of the most popular iPhone apps—a percentage that was continuing to decline—were available on the Blackberry platform. He also realized that the technologically amazing new Android and Windows smartphones would continue to provide vigorous competition to the struggling Research in Motion, Blackberry's parent company, in the coming months and years. He even understood that many, if not most, professional analysts around the world were taking an increasingly dim view of Research in Motion's long-term financial viability.

Perhaps it was simply a matter of laziness. Changing phones seemed like a monumental waste of time and effort.

Or maybe it had something to do with the overwhelming power of habit. Like many private club members around the world—and certainly *all* Senior Members—Clive wasn't particularly enthralled with change of *any* kind. No, it was neither of these things, Clive knew in the darkest recesses of his still-fertile and creative mind. The real reason why he still doggedly clung to his Blackberry was the keyboard. When you thumb-type a text or an e-mail on a Blackberry, the letters and numbers actually *depress*. Clive liked that. He liked that a lot. *How depressing that more people don't know the true joy of depressing!* The fancy-dancy touchscreen keyboards of the so-called competition just didn't work for him; his apparently "fatter than normal" thumbs always caused him to make far more typographical errors than he thought any reasonable person ever need make. *No, let the disloyal rats abandon ship if they must. If necessary, Blackberry's captain and I will go down together, arm in arm, to our watery graves, thumb-typing grammatically and syntactically correct messages to the last on keys that depress.*

Clive glanced at the digital clock atop his matching Edwardian dresser—like his bed, the pristine antique still boasted the original distinctive walnut grain and lustrous patination—and saw that it was one twenty-nine in the morning. Most of him wanted to collapse back into bed and let sleep's welcome refuge have its way, but a nagging voice in the far corner of his always-responsible left brain pressed him to check his phone. A text at this ungodly hour simply did not make sense.

Clive saw quickly that he had received two texts from Esther. *Of course. Esther! Who* else *would it be!* The first, which had come about an hour and a half ago, was her typical über-polite, well-crafted response to the message he had carefully thumb-typed earlier in the day. It was clear she was continuing to thoroughly enjoy herself in New Zealand. The picture she had attached, though certainly not up to the lofty standards of a professional photographer, did succeed in intimating the stark beauty and majestic splendor of The Remarkables.

The second text, the one that he had just received, was startlingly un-Esther-like in both its wording and length. It said only, "Hello, boss. Esther here. Please give me a call when convenient."

Knowing it was five thirty in the evening in New Zealand, and given the fact that he was now (unfortunately) stone-cold-sober awake, Clive decided to call Esther right away. Besides, it must be something really important if she actually wanted to *talk*, not just communicate by text or e-mail. *I'm not really sure* anyone *under the age of twenty actually knows how to talk.* Esther answered before the second ring had ended.

"Thank you for calling me back so quickly, boss. I figured you were asleep and would get back to me in the morning. I am so sorry if my text woke you," said Esther contritely. "I was thinking that your cell would be switched to silent for the night."

"No worries, Esther. I was awake anyway and somehow forgot to switch off my Blackberry before going to bed. When I read your second text, I decided to call you right back. So tell me, what's so important that we need to speak?"

"Boss, get this. I just saw Mr. Tumorington! He snuck up behind me after I left the Skyline Gondola and was walking back to my car. He looks awful, like he has aged twenty years. The harsh realities of prison life have obviously taken their dire toll."

"Are you *okay*, Esther? He didn't try to hurt you, did he?" an alarmed Clive nearly shouted back. *Typical Esther, worrying about how a former Old Bunbury member and now convicted murderer on the run from the law looked rather than considering her own personal safety.*

"Relax, boss. I am fine. Really. However, I have to tell you that Mr. Tumorington *did* tell me, in no uncertain terms, that he was going to get even for what I did to him back at Old Bunbury—you know, helping Detective Giztips and the police prove that he was the one who murdered Mr. Johnson. Mr. Tumorington threatened my life, boss! However, he also stressed that he would take his 'rightful retribution'—those were his exact words—'on United States soil,' not here in New Zealand. It all happened so fast; the entire encounter couldn't have lasted more than a minute. Before I knew it, he had vanished into thin air. I was, I must admit, shaken up at first, but I am now starting to feel a bit better. I'm back at my hotel and sitting in the bar, surrounded by a large crowd of people. I know Mr. Tumorington won't bother me here. I'm safe for now. I really am."

"I am going to call Detective Giztips and ask him what we should do," said an obviously still-shaken Clive.

"No, please don't do that, boss," said Esther calmly, "at least not until morning. I very much believe what Mr. Tumorington said about his not attempting to harm me while I remain in New Zealand. Besides, it would be far too risky. It's already Thursday evening here, and my flight home leaves Christchurch on Sunday afternoon. I have less than three days left in this spectacularly beautiful and wonderfully friendly country, and I am going to enjoy, to the very best of my ability, every single minute."

"Alright, Esther. Most of that that sounds reasonable to me. One thing, however, is for certain; I *am* going to call Detective Giztips immediately and report what just happened. I am quite sure that the appropriate authorities, both here in the United States and in New Zealand, will want to know this critically important information concerning Hamish's whereabouts as soon as possible," Clive continued, his voice regulating with each passing moment. "The fact that he is in central Queenstown, or at least was as of twenty minutes ago, narrows Hamish's general location a great deal. This can only help increase the chances for a successful capture. I am confident that the New Zealand authorities will be most cooperative with America's ongoing efforts to apprehend an escaped and apparently now-maniacal convicted murderer hell-bent on revenge."

"Thank you, boss. Yes, that is the right thing to do. Detective Giztips will surely appreciate hearing from you, even at this ghastly hour."

"Are you sure you are okay, Esther?" Clive asked, the deep concern in his voice not lost on her.

"I'm fine, boss. Really. I have to tell you, though, that when I was with Mr. Tumorington, a sort of eerie, atavistic chill oozed down the entire length of my spine. He was actually grinning, boss—taking, I think, a sort of perverse pleasure in what was happening. It reminded me of one of those demonic, irrational smiles you see in an old Freddy Krueger movie. Almost inhuman. It was as if he had rehearsed exactly what he was going to say to me. I don't know, boss; perhaps he did. Then again, maybe I am over-analyzing all of this. Like I said, the whole encounter happened so quickly."

"Look, Esther, you watch out for yourself the next three days. I mean it. Be *very* careful; don't take any unnecessary chances. Wherever you go and whatever you do, make sure that other people, and ideally, *lots* of other people, are always around. I'll get back to you after I speak with Detective Giztips. My guess is that he will want to contact you as well. Assuming he does, I'll ask him to get in touch with you tomorrow morning, your time."

"Thanks, boss. I appreciate all that you are doing. After you speak with Detective Giztips, I suggest that you try to get some sleep. I'm going to have that snack and glass of Chardonnay to help calm my jangled nerves. I won't be long out of bed, myself."

It is a little known fact that the Obama administration has been secretly funding the South Island sheep-cabal's nefarious plan to wrest political control from the human residents.

Chapter 18

Esther's Final Three Days

If Esther's pace during the first ten days of her current New Zealand visit had approached frenetic, her final three in the country clearly crossed the line. She was fiercely determined to put the unpleasant, potentially discombobulating encounter with a certain Hamish P. Tumorington out of her mind and to focus instead on savoring her remaining time in her beloved Aotearoa. Esther, whatever her many foibles and idiosyncrasies, was wise enough to know that the busier she kept with travel and sightseeing, the less time she would have to dwell on the near-frightening, retributive threats from the former Old Bunbury member and now-convicted murderer on the loose.

Detective Adam Giztips, the talented and caring young officer from the metropolitan police with whom she had so well "teamed" to solve the Alfie Johnson murder case not all that many years ago, had indeed spoken with Esther not long after she had gotten out of bed on Friday morning. Ever the perfect combination of efficient policeman and courteous gentleman, the good detective had first sent her a gracious text message requesting a specific time when they might talk.

Their conversation had lasted well over an hour. Detective Giztips had carefully, methodically prompted her to regurgitate as many details of her brief but alarming encounter with Hamish as humanly possible. He had been thorough and meticulous in this regard, and Esther had striven to answer each and every one of his comprehensive and probing questions to the very best of her ability. Esther knew from her previous experience with Detective Giztips that every detail, no matter how seemingly small, trivial, or unrelated, might very well prove to be of significant value at some later time.

Finally, when Detective Giztips had been satisfied that he had garnered all the relevant information he could, the veteran policeman had reiterated the importance of her remaining "extra vigilant" for her remaining days in New Zealand. Specifically, Detective Giztips seconded Clive's good advice about avoiding places where there were few or no other people. He also reported that the appropriate authorities in the United States had already spoken with those in New Zealand about her recent unanticipated run-in with Hamish P. Tumorington and that, as expected, all parties had been most cooperative. He also confirmed that, just as soon the two of them had finished with their conversation, he would relay all that he had learned to his superiors. Finally, Detective Giztips had promised to meet with Esther in person as soon she returned to the United States.

Esther visited a variety of scenic places and wonderful attractions, both natural and man-made, over the course of her last three days on the South Island. Many, she had seen before—for Esther, second and third visits were typically richer, deeper learning opportunities that confirmed and enhanced what she had previously experienced—but, this time, two of the three were first time stops. The first of these first-time stops was Slope Point.

Slope Point, as Esther had long known, is the southernmost point of the South Island. In the United States, such a geographical oddity would certainly have long been exploited by all sorts of cheesy souvenir shops, second-rate hotels, aging video arcades, and fast-food chains. In typical New Zealand fashion, however, the land around Slope Point was still privately owned, dedicated specifically to nothing other than sheep farming, and had no houses or buildings of any kind nearby. In point of fact, there is no paved road at all to Slope Point; to reach it, one must make a twenty-or-so–minute walk following dilapidated, sparsely placed, hard-to-find markers. To further confuse the situation, there is no public access during the lambing season; sheep *rule* on the South Island.

Esther, doing her best to adhere to the good advice of both Detective Giztips and President Ogive, remained locked in her Camry in the tiny, barely noticeable Slope Point automobile pull-off for almost thirty minutes before another vehicle containing two more intrepid, off-the-beaten-path adventurers appeared on the horizon. She carefully monitored the slow approach of the thirtiesh-looking, long-haired couple for more than half a mile, so by the time they had also arrived and parked their ten-year-old cadet-blue Ford Fiesta, she knew for certain that Hamish P. Tumorington was nowhere to be found. *Well, it is not a* lot *of other people, but I am certainly not foolish enough to make this walk alone. However, I* am *going to see Slope Point!*

Following brief introductions—they were John and Mary Smith, on holiday from Rotorua on the North Island—the three made the purposely slow, comfortably silent stroll to the remote, hauntingly beautiful tip of the South Island, a place marked by nothing more than a weather-worn yellow sign, remarkable only in its ordinariness for such a geographically significant location. The spitting rain and blustery winds that accompanied their slow trek on the unpaved, rutted muddy trail somehow made the rugged isolation and stark beauty of the place all the more surreal. They could very well have been the last three people alive on good planet Earth. It was an experience, Esther knew, that none of the three would ever forget. *I certainly won't forget two people with such strange names!*

Esther's second first-time visit—this one on late Saturday morning—was to Olveston, the bustling little university city of Dunedin's most famous, and perhaps most historic, home. For reasons long-forgotten, she had missed seeing this one-of-a-kind little gem on her previous visits to the South Island.

The Jacobean-style house, Esther soon learned, had been built by one David Theomin, a financially successful, socially privileged businessman who had named his new Dunedin dwelling in honor of the little village from which he had originally emigrated in South Gloucestershire, England. After more than two years of planning, design, and construction, David; his young wife, Marie; son, Edward; and daughter, Dorothy, had proudly moved into their grand new residence in 1906. The thirty-five room mansion is distinguished by its wealth of architectural detail and irreplaceable collection of high-end art and artifacts collected by David and his family during their several decades of extensive world travel. When daughter Dorothy, the sole surviving member of the family, had passed away in 1966, Olveston and its contents had been generously bequeathed to the city. In the ensuing years, the thoughtful combination of carefully researched replication, restoration, and conservation had made the home a must-see for anyone visiting the South Island's second largest city.

For reasons unknown, the Olveston estate captured Esther's soul. She and her most knowledgeable and gracious guide—Esther, as it happened, was the only visitor on this rainy, bone-chilling morning, so she had the good docent all to herself—spent close to two hours happily roaming from room to room, soaking in the eclectic display of one-of-a-kind treasures garnered over time from the far reaches of the earth. There were stunningly beautiful original watercolors, oil paintings, and graphic designs; an extensive assemblage of Chinese jades, ceramics, pottery, and fine porcelains; a daunting array of eighteenth- and nineteenth-century Japanese weaponry; and a varied assortment of custom-designed European and American antique furniture. Esther, qua culinary connoisseur, was particularly fascinated by the unusually large kitchen. At the time the home was built, the kitchen had been truly a state-of-the-art masterpiece that featured a sizeable custom-designed cooking range boasting both a roasting oven for meats, chicken, and fish and a baking oven for breads, cakes, and pies. An ample collection of Delft-style pottery filled the massive kauri-wood tables and dressers lining the decoratively tiled walls. The Theomin family, in addition to being magnanimously philanthropic, had clearly also not been shy about spending considerably to personally enjoy the finer things of life. *Good for them!* Her next trip to the South Island, Esther silently vowed as she left the meticulously manicured grounds, would surely warrant a return visit to this fascinating, historic, and expertly preserved old home.

Esther's third and final visit occurred on Sunday morning in Christchurch, this trip's point of arrival and also the city from which she would begin her long journey back to the United States later that same afternoon. This encore visit was to the International Antarctic Centre. It was, she knew, the perfect place at which to end this particular New Zealand journey. Not only was it conveniently situated adjacent to the airport, but its focus on bringing its visitors a comprehensive, powerful, and memorable experience about the Antarctic—with its emphasis on informing them about many of the same penguin species that also inhabited the southern coastlines of New Zealand—provided an especially fitting way for Esther to end her latest South Island odyssey.

Esther purchased the Xtreme Entry Pass—the purposeful misspelling made her physically cringe—entitling her to take in the Penguin Encounter, the Snow and Ice Experience, the Simulated Antarctic Storm, the 4D Extreme Theatre, and the ten-minute Hagglund Tractor Ride (the amazing all-terrain amphibious vehicle developed and used by those who chose to live in and explore the bottom of the world). It was difficult for her to say which attraction she enjoyed most. By the time she had finished with her visit, Esther felt that she had gained a significantly better understanding of the mind-boggling vastness of the Antarctic's polar plateau and all that it entailed. She certainly would unconditionally recommend a visit to the International Antarctic Centre to anyone who would listen.

Within twenty-five minutes of leaving the International Antarctic Centre, Esther had successfully returned her Camry—a procedure that, happily, turned out to be noticeably less cumbersome that picking it up—checked in at the airline counter and had her luggage correctly tagged to her final destination, and made her way to the point beyond which only confirmed passengers were allowed to enter. Whether by pure happenstance or some primordial form of woman's intuition, Esther cast a quick glance over her shoulder, perhaps nothing more than a final fleeting, bittersweet tribute to all that she had experienced these past two weeks. There, no farther than thirty yards away, stood a grinning, waving Hamish P. Tumorington, looking for all the world like he were witnessing the departure of his own mother on a long-overdue extended vacation. Gasping, Esther purposely closed her eyes for at least three full seconds, convinced that her overactive imagination was playing some sort of horribly twisted trick. When she finally mustered up the courage to reopen them and force a second look, there was no Hamish to be seen. *You are seeing things, Esther! Get a grip!*

Less than an hour later, a still semi-rattled Esther was comfortably seated in her first-class seat and more than ready to begin the long journey home.

The rugged isolation and stark beauty of Slope Point stirs something deep and profound in Esther's caring soul.

Part II

The United States

Chapter 19

Home, but Not Alone

Esther made the physically exhausting but mentally comforting twenty-seven–hour trek back to her base airport in the United States without incident. As much as she adored her whirlwind, activity-packed excursions to her beloved New Zealand, Esther also knew that there is something quite magical about returning home. Esther just wished that, like Dorothy, she could have simply thrice clicked the heels of her ruby slippers to eliminate all that boring intervening travel time. *Then again, I don't own any ruby slippers. Never have, never will.*

Though Esther had tried her best not to think about Hamish P. Tumorington and the lethal harm he had so ominously threatened—twice, she had become totally convinced after a full day of continuing rumination—she could not fully dismiss either of the foreboding encounters from her still-racing mind. One can, Esther knew better than most, watch only so many movies, read so many books, play so many games, take so many catnaps, consume so much food, and drink so many glasses of Chardonnay on an airplane. All that time left alone with one's thoughts, no matter how luxurious it might be in first class—and, Esther had to admit, it was indeed quite luxurious traversing the Pacific in seat 3B—was not exactly conducive to preventing one's mind from wandering into those darker recesses better left untraveled. Having too much time on one's hands is *never* a good thing. Ironically, perhaps Esther was experiencing a mini-inkling of what Hamish had encountered during his stint in prison. *No, don't even begin to feel sorry for that heinous murderer. Hamish P. Tumorington brought it all upon himself and deserved exactly what he got!*

After quickly passing through customs and successfully retrieving her three stylishly matched pieces of Pierre Cardin luggage, Esther methodically made her way out of the more heavily secured passenger-only area into the recently remodeled main section of the terminal. There, to her considerable surprise—and, if truth be told, her great pleasure as well—stood both President Clive Endive Ogive IV and Detective Adam Giztips.

"Hello, Esther. Welcome home," beamed an effusive, smiling Clive, leaning forward to give her a chaste, longtime friend–to–longtime friend hug. "I assume your flights all went as scheduled?" he asked.

"Yes, boss, they did. Right on time. Thank you for asking. If I may be so blunt, what in heaven's name are you two doing here? I left my car parked in the long-term garage right across the street." Turning, Esther extended her steady hand to Adam Giztips. "Hello, Detective Giztips. So very nice to see you. It's been a while."

"Yes, Esther, it has," said an also grinning Adam Giztips, clasping Esther's extended right hand in a hearty shake. It was difficult to tell which of the three was most pleased. "Clive and I agreed it best to meet you personally," he continued, speaking for the both of them. "We know, of course, that the odds of Hamish attempting to do you any harm here in the airport are extremely unlikely. The truth be told, Esther, Hamish is but a feeble excuse for our being here; we both wanted to personally greet our favorite New Zealand adventurer upon her return to the United States."

"Well, that is so very nice of the both of you. I am indeed one lucky lady to count two such dapper, good-looking, and intelligent gentlemen among my inner circle of friends," said a genuinely grateful Esther.

"So," Esther continued after several seconds of comfortable mutual silence, "is there any news regarding Mr. Tumorington's whereabouts?" It had crossed Esther's mind more than once during her long journey home that perhaps Lady Luck had successfully partnered with the considerable sleuthing skills of the good detectives from both the United States and New Zealand to produce the capture of one Hamish P. Tumorington.

"Nothing," they said in unison, the disappointment evident in their tones of voice as well as their body language. Detective Giztips continued for the two, "It's as if Hamish has vanished into thin air. To be honest, we don't have a lot to go on, other than your one brief encounter with our revenge-seeking escaped murderer in the center of Queenstown. We have no clue as to what alias he might be traveling under, what route he plans to take back to the United States, nor even when he plans to return."

"I have to tell you both something," said an uncharacteristically sheepish Esther. "I believe that I saw Mr. Tumorington at the Christchurch airport shortly before my first airplane departed. I didn't report it before my jet took off because, at the time, I was convinced that an overactive imagination had been playing some sort of cruel trick on me. When I uncovered my stunned eyes and gathered the courage to take a second look, he was nowhere to be seen."

"Well, that is indeed disconcerting news, Esther," said an anxious Detective Giztips. "If I may say, you are a fiercely determined and incredibly perceptive young woman, so let me pose this question: *If* you had to say, now having had over a full day to carefully ponder what is so obviously a deeply unsettling matter, do you believe, in your heart of hearts, that Hamish was actually there at the Christchurch airport with you?"

"I may be getting up there in years, Detective, but my mind, I still like to believe, remains as sharp and focused as ever," Esther answered, her defiant tone daring either of them to contradict her purposefully determined words. "No, I thought a *lot* about it on my plane rides home, and I am now fully convinced that Mr. Tumorington, in all his mentally unstable malevolence, was really standing no further than thirty yards away from me, if only for a few seconds, just as I was about to enter the passenger-only section of the Christchurch airport."

"This second encounter with Mr. Tumorington," Esther continued after a bit, "I must tell you, was especially strange and disturbing; he just stood there, smiling and waving at me, as if he were some longtime personal friend who had made a special trip to the airport just to see me off. To tell you the truth, seeing Mr. Tumorington in this eerie context was all the more ominous and frightening. I tried to convince myself on the plane ride home that my imagination had played some sort of nefarious trick on me, but to no avail; I know for certain that the incident was real. Yes, Hamish P. Tumorington was surely there at the Christchurch airport, if only briefly—and that is why I am now telling you this."

"I understand," said a sympathetic Detective Giztips. "I will immediately report to my superiors what you have just told me, but I don't hold out much hope of our apprehending Hamish based solely upon this new information. It's been over twenty-eight hours since you last saw him; by now, Hamish could be literally anywhere in the world."

"Boss," said Esther, abruptly changing the conversation, a skill at which no one was more adept, "I am very anxious to get back to work. I feel confident that Old Bunbury, where I will be surrounded by the wonderful members and outstanding staff, will surely be one of the safer places for me to be in the entire world. Besides, it's been over two weeks since the members have had the opportunity to experience the world-class service for which I am so justifiably well known," deadpanned Esther, the wry smile on her face not unnoticed by her two fellow conversationalists.

"We will be happy to have you back at work, Esther, although perhaps for reasons other than what you have just articulated," answered Clive diplomatically.

"I agree with Esther," said Detective Giztips, doing his best to ignore the obviously good-natured gamesmanship between the two longtime Mutt-and-Jeff friends. "Indeed, Old Bunbury is probably one of the better places for Esther at this point in time. We'll be able to keep a close watch on her every move and, as we all know, nonmembers and guests at Old Bunbury are more conspicuous than Barack Obama at a meeting of the John Birch Society." (To Clive, Adam, Esther, and anyone with an intelligence quotient above eighty-two, colonoscopies, pancreatitis, and head lice are preferable to Obama.)

Turning to face Esther, Detective Giztips continued, "I do have one request, Esther. I would like you to meet with me tomorrow morning at my office, say around ten, to carefully recount the details of your two harrowing encounters with Hamish. As you well know from our previous work together, people can and do often recall additional facts the second time they recite a story, tidbits of previously forgotten information that sometimes turn out to be critically important to the successful solving of a case. Does this work for you?"

"Yes, Detective, indeed it does. I will tell you absolutely everything I remember tomorrow morning."

"Thank you, Esther," said Adam Giztips. "I want you to know that the police are taking Hamish's threat to your well-being *very* seriously. Accordingly, we are going to assign you twenty-four–hour surveillance. You will have a trained security officer watching over you—as unobtrusively as possible, of course—at all times. Please rest assured that we are going to do everything we can to capture this heinous convicted murderer as soon as humanly possible. Candidly, while we currently have no clue as to Hamish's whereabouts, we are not going to take any chances whatsoever when it comes to your personal safely."

"Thank you, Detective," cooed an obviously grateful Esther.

"One last point, Esther," said Detective Giztips. "While both Clive and I have the utmost respect for your considerable sleuthing powers—skills that were confirmed and enhanced when you and I worked together not all that long ago—neither of us will tolerate your attempting to 'solve' Hamish's whereabouts by yourself." The unwavering resoluteness in his deep voice was not lost on her. "Besides," he added, purposely mellowing his tone, "for some strange reason, both Clive and I are quite fond of you. I am well aware that, when it comes to Old Bunbury, absolutely *no one* knows more than you. Therefore, if and when a potential idea regarding Hamish's whereabouts enters your especially fertile and inquisitive mind, I expect that you will notify me immediately."

"Indeed I will," answered a somber Esther. "I certainly have no desire to take up permanent residence in the great private club in the sky, at least for the foreseeable future. This feisty woman still has a lot to do and see in her remaining years on good planet Earth."

"Excellent. Now would you please guide us to your car, Esther?" asked Clive, picking up the largest of Esther's three pieces of obviously expensive designer luggage. "I will drive you home, and Detective Giztips will meet us there with your assigned security officer. I have no doubt that you are quite exhausted."

Are these merely blissful sheep innocently grazing in their home meadow, or are they part of the rumored South Island ovine coup d'état?

Chapter 20

Esther's Return to Old Bunbury

Esther's two-hour meeting with Detective Giztips the following morning, though grueling and intense, was also indisputably productive. As was his custom with highly cooperative eyewitnesses, Detective Giztips was patient and kind in his questioning, but thorough and persistent as well. His considerable professional skills were on full display as he coaxed and cajoled every possible detail out of Esther with regard to her two New Zealand encounters with Hamish P. Tumorington. After carefully eliciting, clarifying, and recording all the thoughts and impressions he deemed even remotely potentially relevant, Detective Giztips became as convinced as Esther that Hamish's appearance at the Christchurch airport was not some sort of hapless mental illusion on her part. As the session approached its welcome conclusion, Esther, though grateful to Detective Giztips for his excellent interrogatory work, was emotionally spent and intellectually exhausted.

"Well, that will do it for now, Esther," Detective Giztips said at long last. "I sincerely appreciate your complete, candid, and uncensored testimony. I only wish that everyone I am required to interview demonstrated your considerable abilities of recall and attention to detail. I know these past couple of hours have been quite taxing for you, but both of us understand, far better than most, that the exercise was a necessary one. While I am not certain if we have garnered any new nuggets of information that will directly expedite Hamish's capture, we can only remain positive. Perhaps my superiors and I will find something useful and revealing amidst the myriad details that you have so painstakingly provided. Thank you again, Esther."

"Thank *you*, Detective," answered a genuinely grateful Esther. "You know that I am always ready and willing to help the police—and that, I might add, applies doubly for *you*. No one, I can assure you, wants Mr. Tumorington promptly returned to prison more than I. Now, if you don't mind, I am going to head over to Old Bunbury to say hello to some members and employees. It's been over two weeks since I was last at the club, and a *lot* has happened during the intervening time. I may even wait on a table or two."

"I am sure everyone at Old Bunbury will unconditionally appreciate such a magnanimous offer on your part," said Detective Giztips, doing his best to remain straight-faced, but not quite succeeding. Given the right circumstances, Adam Giztips could be as sardonic as the best. "Please be sure to drive safely and at an appropriate pace at all times," he continued, once again his serious professional self. "Remember, you will have a trained security officer nearby at all times."

Indeed, Esther arrived at Old Bunbury during the peak of the lunch hour "rush." (For a club so private and exclusive as Old Bunbury, the rush, even at the height of season, was never more than seven or eight tables.) In typical Esther fashion, she did absolutely nothing to announce her arrival, completely oblivious to the fact that her absence for the past sixteen days might be conspicuous or noteworthy in any way. Instead, Esther strode purposefully through the front door of the clubhouse and, after deftly inventorying the members seated around the main dining room and quickly identifying the table she liked best—that is, the one that would cause the least ruckus and submit the simplest order—she was ready to begin her work. Only an unexpected gentle tap on her right shoulder by longtime club manager Jay Morris prevented her from proceeding.

"Hello, Esther," said Jay. "So happy to see you made it back to the United States unscathed. One of these days, I plan on visiting New Zealand myself, but that is a conversation for another day."

"Hello, Jay," bubbled Esther. "It surely is great to be back at the best private club in the entire world."

Sensing that Esther remained intent on "helping" with the main dining room table service, Jay promptly continued, "Please rest assured that there is no need for your to take any orders at this time. The other servers, I am confident, will do their dutiful best to muddle through without your expert guidance," deadpanned the ever-diplomatic club manager. Jay's ability to always say the right thing at the right time—no matter what he really thought—was but one of the many diverse personal and professional skills that had led to his unusually long and respected tenure in the private club management industry. "If you don't mind, President Ogive and I would like to see you for a few minutes in my office. He's sitting at my desk."

"Certainly," said Esther suspiciously. "Is there something wrong?"

"To the contrary, Esther," Jay answered. "The entire membership and staff is absolutely delighted to learn that you have returned from your latest adventures in New Zealand safe and sound, especially in light of your harrowing encounters with our now-infamous and internationally wanted former member. We just want to fill you in on one or two things about which you may not yet be aware. Of course, I know full well that, in short order, you would have discovered everything that we are about to tell you."

"Hello, Esther," said Clive Endive Ogive IV as Jay and Esther entered Jay's cramped and disheveled office. Jay Morris was one of those people whose skills at filing, sorting, and arranging appeared on the surface to be marginal, but if prompted, he could and would—and at a moment's notice—locate any and all requested documents amidst the randomly appearing piles strewn across the room. Jay was living proof that, for some, even gross disorder is a type of order.

"Hello, boss. Thank you again for meeting me at the airport late yesterday afternoon. It meant a lot to me. You may have already heard, but I just finished a marathon questioning session with Detective Giztips. He certainly is one *very* talented and knowledgeable law-enforcement official. I am quite convinced he elicited and recorded every possible detail about my two encounters with Mr. Tumorington. To be honest, I am not sure that we discovered anything additional that will prove of significant or immediate help, but you never know. So what's new?"

"You would have found out soon enough on your own, Esther, but Jay and I want to tell you firsthand about this morning's specially called session of the Old Bunbury Board of Directors. We met secretly at a discreet site away from the club," said Clive.

"Yes, I did hear that the group was gathering at Mr. Swank's newly remodeled guesthouse. Too bad that Mrs. McFarlane Whitestone was out of town on critical Pillow Committee work and unable to attend," said Esther.

"It figures," muttered Clive stoically. Nothing, absolutely nothing, surprised him when it came to Esther's encyclopedic knowledge of all things Old Bunbury. *I wouldn't be surprised if she knew exactly how each and every Roman Catholic cardinal from around the world voted in the most recent papal conclave.*

"Anyway," Clive continued, though it was apparent that he was still somewhat shaken, "you may not yet know all the details of what the group decided, so let me fill you in. After a fair amount of discussion, the consensus opinion of the board was that it makes good sense for a number of excellent reasons, not the least of which, I might add, is your personal safety, to have you back at Old Bunbury working your normal hours—whatever the term 'normal' might mean in your case," added Clive, turning to Jay for help. Getting only a befuddled shrug, Clive quickly pressed on. "The board also approved the confidential hiring of a new sous chef, a position that, coincidentally, Jay has been trying to fill for some time. The good news is that, as it now happens, our new assistant cook is a retired law-enforcement officer and someone who has agreed to secretly attend to your safety when you are on the club grounds. In the interest of preventing any disruption to our club's normal great service to the membership, we ask that you keep your knowledge of this fact totally confidential. Only Jay, I, and a few key members of the board know that our new sous chef has the talent, desire, and temperament to accept this added responsibility."

"Thank you, boss," said a grateful Esther. "That is very much appreciated. "Just out of curiosity, can our new sous chef actually cook?"

"Actually, yes, Esther," answered Jay for the both of them. "After retiring from police work, Old Bunbury's latest employee started a second career—quite successfully, I have recently learned—in the wonderful world of the culinary arts. Detective Giztips is quite comfortable with this arrangement and, in fact, enthusiastically supports the board's approach to the matter of your safety and protection. Of course, when you are away from Old Bunbury, you will, as previously discussed, have an active police officer nearby. President Ogive and Detective Giztips talked this through late yesterday evening and agreed that, all things considered, this was the best solution to the issue at hand." After a few seconds of silence, Jay concluded with, "So, do you have any questions, Esther?"

"Not at this time, gentlemen. I wholeheartedly agree that it is in the overall interests of the club to keep this information on a need-to-know basis, and you can certainly rest assured that I will tell nary a soul. None of us wants any interruptions whatsoever to the normal traditions and customs of our great club," said a grateful Esther.

"Thank you for understanding and cooperating," said a relieved Jay Morris. "Just so you know, Esther, our new sous chef—his name is Morris Less—will be working the breakfast and lunch shifts. Accordingly, I would appreciate your adhering to your past record of not working nights. You might even consider showing up for work on those lunch shifts at which you are actually scheduled, as this would make things a lot easier on all of us."

"That is a fair enough request, Jay," hedged Esther. "I haven't worked the dinner shift in over a decade, and I don't plan on starting now. At this particular stage of my life, my evenings have a higher calling: reading, relaxing, and savoring fine Chardonnays. I will also do my best to adhere to the posted schedule, although, as always, I do retain the right to remain flexible. That, as you both well know, is just who I am."

"Your best efforts in this regard are all that we can reasonably expect," said a resigned Jay Morris. He knew from long experience that to push any further was a losing battle. "Now let's go meet Morris. Following that, I am sure that the members and staff currently on property will want to say hello and hear about your latest adventures. More than a few, I have heard, are greatly relieved that your most recent trip overseas did not lead to an international incident."

Jay Morris is universally acknowledged as one of the private club industry's most accomplished and caring general managers.

Chapter 21

A Good-Enough Shot

Although she was no longer a crack marksman—in her salad days, Esther could nail a slender-tailed meerkat in its left ass cheek at fifty paces—she could still hit her chosen part of a small torso, if and when the need should ever arise, with each of her three remaining firearms. Unbeknownst to anyone else now alive, Esther's strikingly handsome, exceedingly kind, and ever-optimistic father had immersed her, as a very young girl, in the proper care, dutiful respect, and correct handling of guns of all kind. Throughout the vicissitudes of her long and extremely interesting life, munitions expertise had remained something that Esther had never abandoned, had always cherished, and regularly honed. Many decades ago, Esther had, with minimal fanfare, obtained her concealed weapons permit. For several years, she actually had carried a firearm more often than not. In fact, Esther had continued to faithfully renew her license to this day—a valid concealed weapons permit was a prized possession that she would proudly take to her grave. For reasons long forgotten, Esther had gradually gotten out of the habit of carrying a concealed weapon of any sort, something that, as an American, she had every right to do. Perhaps, with Mr. Tumorington on the lam and hell-bent on the ultimate revenge, it was now time for her to reconsider that antiquated life decision.

At this point in her life, Esther's personal arsenal had been purposely reduced to just three firearms. She owned two pistols, the classic Smith & Wesson K-Frame Model 65 revolver—a stainless-steel Magnum .357 that had once been the standard issue of many police departments around the United States—and a Smith & Wesson Model 39, a semiautomatic, double-action pistol renowned for its performance, sleek beauty, and ease-of-use. Esther had also kept, primarily for sentimental reasons, her original Winchester Model 70 rifle, the perfect high-school graduation gift from her doting father all those decades ago. It was a gun that, because of its pure grace, unquestioned reliability, and pinpoint accuracy (at least for its time), was invariably included in everyone's short list of the greatest rifles of all time.

Esther had always been baffled by the gross naiveté, irrational fear, and childlike gullibility of many, if not most, liberals when it came to guns. She found the far left's renewed illogical, no-holds-barred assault upon the sacred Second Amendment to the United States Constitution clear confirmation that so many Americans no longer studied nor valued the glorious history of a country founded upon the individual core liberties and inalienable rights of its citizenry. *Whatever happened to "Give me liberty or give me death," Patrick's Henry's once famous life-guiding patriotic rallying cry for generations of knowledgeable, freedom-loving Americans everywhere?*

Interestingly, Esther knew that conservatives, at their core, were generally driven and guided by history, logic, facts, and the truth while diehard liberals (sadly) were typically not. When the far left's grossly distorted worldview and accompanying gobbledygook policies were quickly exposed and readily refuted—something that Rush Limbaugh has continued to do with dazzling eloquence, devastating logic, and understated humor for over a quarter of a century—the ovine Marxist faithful immediately turned to their hackneyed playbook of ad hominem attacks, gross distortions, circumvention of the accepted rules of civil behavior, guilt tripping, reframing of the issues, ecological extortion and environmental blackmail, bare-faced lies, and infantile emotional appeals. The ends, no matter how inappropriate and vile, always justified the means. The attempted gutting of the Second Amendment by Barack Hussein Obama and his dastardly minions—and, as Esther and millions of others well knew, their mutually supporting attacks on a host of other fundamentally important individual civil rights issues as well—was downright un-American and unprecedented in her wonderful country's long and distinguished history. Obama, if truth be told, was nothing more than a woefully incompetent leader and skillfully brazen liar shamelessly propped up by a conspiring radical media and enabled by the denigration and disintegration of a distinctly American culture. *If they put someone in jail for unmitigated arrogance, overt disdain for America's core guiding principles, and a blatant inability to govern, Barack Hussein Obama and his inner circle would be serving life sentences without parole.*

Esther knew that, in the end, the ultimate, unstated goal of the uppity far left was to take away Americans' right to bear arms of any kind; everything else, especially the emotionally charged appeals to "safety" and "reduced street violence," were nothing more than cheap pandering and political posturing. (Esther certainly knew that not all liberals were ill-intentioned or inherently evil. Many, if not most, were probably good, sincere, law-abiding—although naive and foolish—people who were truly unaware, for whatever reason or reasons, about all that had made America the world's beacon of individual rights and freedoms for the previous two and a half centuries. The truly evil ones, Esther knew, were those co-conspiring, so-called intellectuals and elites of the governmental ruling class who, like power-grabbers the world over, wanted to concentrate more and more power in the controlling hands of fewer and fewer. *These* were the diabolical cadre fiendishly plotting to take away Americans' constitutionally guaranteed right to bear arms—people who didn't give a yellow-bellied marmot's shinbone what the vast majority of Americans wanted and thought.)

Esther, like tens of millions of clear-thinking Americans, had been appalled and disgusted at the impudent and brazen exploitation of young and innocent children by Barack Hussein Obama as he pompously inked his twenty-three executive orders further limiting Americans their constitutionally guaranteed access to guns. Anyone with a lick of common sense and passing knowledge of American history knew these orders were clear and egregious violations of the people's core Second Amendment rights. Not only that, Esther also knew that, had *all* twenty-three of these abusive, "politically correct" executive orders been in place the previous year, the tragedy at Sandy Hook Elementary School in Newtown, Connecticut, would still not have been prevented. To the diehard left, Sandy Hook was nothing more than a welcome opportunity to craft and cram unwanted policies crafted by a ruling minority down the throats of the majority of powerless, unwilling Americans. Obama's inane executive gun-control mandates, Esther so well knew, were analogous to trying to reduce drunk driving by making it tougher for sober people to own cars. *How is it that America has come to the point where someone needs a background check to own a gun but not to run a country?*

Esther was horrified and repulsed by a president so condescending and aloof that he remained oblivious to the delicious irony—or, more likely, didn't give a damn about it—of his continuing to haughtily lecture Americans on "the inherent evils of firearms" all from the center of a slew of heavily armed guards. Esther knew that, according to the Federal Bureau of Investigation's own data, more people in the United States were killed each year by baseball bats and knives than guns. Guns were a distant third. *Maybe we should ban Louisville Sluggers.*

Esther also knew that, the more a manipulative, patronizing, know-it-all Barack Hussein Obama and his team of maniacal fear-mongers pressed to disarm Americans under the feeble guise of "safety" and "reduced street violence," the more that tens of millions of clear-thinking, law-abiding citizens would purposely ignore and openly scoff at his unprecedented grab (at least in America) for near-dictatorial power. Only mush-for-brains liberals and the mentally handicapped—a redundancy if there ever was one—would be stupid enough to fall for the fallacious diversionary tactic that America's precious Second Amendment was "really about hunting." There could, Esther knew, be absolutely no legitimate exception to the Second Amendment for military-style weapons, because weaponry of *equal* firepower was an inseparable part of what the Second Amendment guarantees Americans' right to keep and bear. The stated purpose of the Second Amendment is clear: to secure Americans' ability to oppose all enemies, both foreign and domestic—the very guarantee against disorder and tyranny that had helped make the wildly successful American experiment unique the world over. *Why should Americans now be* less *equipped to defend their rights against* anyone *who might seek to take them away?*

No, Esther knew that, at its core, gun control was a supercilious and unconstitutional full-court press by toffee-nosed liberals to remove a core right of the many because of the unfortunate crimes of the few. Esther, like the hundreds of millions of other Americans who so proudly and peacefully resided in all fifty states, was perceptive enough to know that gun control was ultimately not about guns but about control. All gun control would accomplish would be to make it more difficult for the overwhelming majority of good people of the United Stated to successfully defend themselves against the bad; as the old bumper sticker so cleverly stated, "When guns are outlawed, only outlaws will have guns." *Like inner-city Chicago, where only a handful, if that many, of the hundreds of murder victims over the past several years were killed by lawfully registered firearms.* Esther knew, along with virtually every police officer the world over, that the only thing that will ultimately stop a bad guy with a gun is a good guy with a gun. Esther also knew that statistics irrefutably confirmed that gun owners, all things considered, were significantly more law-abiding than the average person on the street. She knew that the more armed a particular citizenry, the fewer crimes were committed. She knew, like her many Canadian friends who proudly owned guns, that the registration of firearms led directly to the confiscation of firearms. It all came down to this: The *logic* for Americans to continue to retain *all* their gun-owning constitutional rights was impeccable and irrefutable—and but one more pathetic example of how the far left, because they cannot win in the world of dispassionate facts, logical discourse, rigorous intellectual debate, and the unfettered truth, must resort to smear tactics, emotional blackmail, straw-man arguments, and outright pernicious lies.

Esther smiled when she remembered the proud gun store owner in Oklahoma who had cleverly awarded Obama "Gun Salesman of the Year"—and with good reason. Gun-store shelves in the past few years had literally been emptied because of Obama's unprecedented, blatantly unconstitutional attempts to disarm Americans. Gun shows, she knew, were regularly setting and breaking attendance records; the more that Obama ranted against the inherent evil of guns, the more that Americans, recognizing his innate buffoonery, caused sales to skyrocket. Gun manufacturers were, more often than not, sold out or back-ordered, with pervasive, ongoing shortages of ammunition and firearms occurring countrywide. *Listen up, Barack Hussein; the American people are speaking and telling you that our Second Amendment rights shall not be infringed.*

Esther's head was spinning from thinking about the utter absurdity of it all. Had her beloved America changed so radically that more people were now concerned with free cell phones than individual core freedoms? *Barack Hussein Obama and his pernicious policy pimp Eric Holder were only too happy to sell automatic weapons to Mexican drug cartels with wanton abandon—but no law-abiding, freedom-loving Americans should have them? What a world!*

Yes, until Hamish was apprehended and once again safely behind locked bars, Esther would begin carrying again. She would tell no one, even though in her heart of hearts, she knew that President Clive, Detective Giztips, and tens of millions of clear-thinking, patriotic, freedom-loving Americans would fully support her decision in this regard.

Sadly, millions of ill-informed liberals, the vast majority of whom have never actually taken the time to read this profoundly important and influential document, are now more intent than ever on destroying it.

Chapter 22

Mr. Steele's Return

Following his lightning-quick, apparition-like encounter with Esther at the Christchurch airport, Mr. Rich V. Steele purposely chose not to set foot on United States soil for another seven days. He knew full well that there was no need to hurry home; when he eventually made his way back, Esther would surely be in the Old Bunbury area, where he could and would execute the next steps of his diabolical plan for revenge accordingly. He also knew that, though he was not being pursued with the same intensity as, say, an international terrorist, the various cooperating national and international police agencies around the world would by now have certainly been notified of his prison escape and at least passively be on the lookout for one Hamish P. Tumorington. The good news was that, to his knowledge, no one had discovered the alias under which he was traveling and that with each passing day, his trail was surely growing colder and interest in his whereabouts waning. Finally, Hamish knew that this was the perfect opportunity to take in a particular part of the world that he had always wanted to visit and see if it would be *the* place he would chose to live once his work with Esther had been completed. *I am once again a free man and will* never, ever *go back to prison!*

Hamish's stateside toadies, in accordance with his master plan of teleological vengeance, had kept him carefully apprised of the movements of Esther, Clive, and the local police during the entire week. He knew, for example, that Esther had safely made it home from New Zealand without setting off an international incident—a possibility, Hamish knew from his decades at Old Bunbury, that one should *never* completely rule out when it came to his former club's loony senior-citizen waitress. He also learned, as he was slowly making his way home, that Esther had met with Detective Giztips at his office the previous Monday morning, presumably to report the details of her encounter with Hamish at the Christchurch airport. Recalling the deer-in-the-headlights look on Esther's face at the time—surely the result of the cat-like nature of his appearance and departure—caused Hamish to think, at least for a time, that she might have actually dismissed the incident as nothing more than a sort of demented mental illusion. He was happy to learn that Esther knew the encounter was real, and pleased that his perfectly timed ghostlike appearance had so unnerved her. *Schadenfreude at its very finest!* Hamish's paid informants had also let him know that Esther was back at work at Old Bunbury—if that were the correct term for what she did at a club he now so deeply reviled for summarily expelling him within weeks after his conviction for the murder of Alfie Johnson. Finally, Hamish learned that the local police had assigned Esther some sort of security detail, at least for the time being. *What a gigantic waste of taxpayer dollars! Okay, not as monumentally idiotic as Obamacare, but a damned close second.*

Hamish's route back to the United States, in accordance with his meticulous master plan, had purposely been a circuitous one. To wit, he left New Zealand three days later than Esther, but instead of returning home the way in which he had come, he continued to head west on his way towards completing an eventual circumnavigation of the globe. Specifically, Hamish took an Emirates Airlines nonstop jumbo jet from Auckland to Dubai, a city that he had always wanted to visit and where, as part of his overall scheme, he spent three wonderfully satisfying days in leisurely exploration. The business-class experience on the exquisitely outfitted new Airbus 380, he had to admit, was second to none.

Hamish had always been fascinated by Dubai, the city-state in the United Arab Emirates that, in an astoundingly few short decades, had emerged from virtually an unknown backwater outpost to a cosmopolitan metropolis that now served as the business center and cultural hub of the Middle East and Persian Gulf region. During his visit to Dubai, Mr. Steele stayed at the luxurious Burj Al Arab, the world's only (self-acclaimed) seven-star hotel. Since its opening in late 1999, the hotel, designed to mimic the mainsail of a ship and situated on an artificial island nearly a thousand feet from the prosperous Jumeirah Beach, had become an icon, if not *the* icon, for the internationally celebrated city-state.

Hamish hired a driver to take him to see the city's highlights. He marveled at the sheer enormity of the Mall of the Emirates, the massive Al Barsha shopping complex featuring five-star hotels, extraordinary attractions, and an impressive array of virtually every major retail chain under the sun. (In what other shopping center, especially one situated in the heart of a desert, could someone find an indoor snow-skiing resort?) He loved driving the length of Palm Jumeirah, the artificial archipelago shaped like a gigantic palm tree jutting out three and a half miles into the water and packed with assorted residential, leisure, and entertainment centers. (Well, one had to put over one hundred million cubic meters of mined sand and rock *someplace*; why not build a new peninsula into the Persian Gulf!) He was fascinated by the Dubai Gold Souk, the traditional market in the heart of Dubai's Deira commercial business district offering its international customers over three hundred retail stores devoted almost exclusively to jewelry. (By most estimates, there were approximately ten *tons* of gold present at any given time in the world-famous souk.) Hamish wandered for more than an hour in and around the towering Burj Khalifa, the recently completed needle-shaped skyscraper that currently reigned as the tallest structure on earth. (If they had tried to erect this twenty-first–century tempered-steel megalith in the United States, it would likely still have been mired down in all sorts of bizarre environmental-impact studies. Heaven help humanity if we wantonly disturb a family of nesting sand crabs!)

If forced to choose, Hamish would have said that his favorite attraction was a far more modest structure, the Dubai Museum. Located in the authentically restored remains of the Al Fahidi Fort, the oldest existing building in the entire city, the museum chronicled and celebrated the traditional way of life in the area before Dubai had morphed into a sort of bizarre hybrid of Manhattan Island and Disney World on steroids.

His Dubai curiosity finally sated by real-life experience—the best kind there is—Hamish flew directly from there to Houston's George Bush International Airport, once again in the luxury of an Emirates Airlines Airbus 380 business-class seat. Mr. Rich V. Steele made it through customs without a hitch—the officer on duty barely gave him a second look—and, after an overnight stay at the nearby Hilton Garden Inn to relax and recuperate, Hamish boarded the final leg of his around-the-world journey the following morning, this time to a second-tier airport two hundred twenty-five miles from his old stomping grounds. Upon landing, Hamish proceeded to rent an innocuous three-year-old light-blue Nissan Sentra from another one of those low-budget agencies a full nine-minute bumpy shuttle ride from the airport terminal—egad!—and carefully, over the course of two days of purposely eschewing the main roads, religiously adhering to the posted speed limits, and carefully blending in with the local traffic patterns, zigzagged his way back to the Old Bunbury area. By the time he checked in to the seedy, family-owned-and-managed motel less than twelve miles from his former favorite private club, he was more than ready to execute the next phase of his fiendishly clever diabolical plan.

Dubai's magnificent Burj Khalifa current reigns as the tallest structure on earth.

Chapter 23

Tuesday's Lunch at the Club

It had been nearly a week since her triumphant return—as Esther's own kindhearted but obviously tainted perspective on the matter would have so worded—to Old Bunbury. She had, much to the pleasant surprise of Jay Morris and the other management staff, adhered to the posted work schedule (well, more or less). That was (technically) the good news. The bad news was that, on those days when it wasn't beneath her to show up for work, Esther still waited on whomever she wanted, whenever she wanted, and, most germane in this case, *if* she wanted. Esther, who had always been picky when it came to actually serving the Old Bunbury membership, had of late been openly avoiding waiting on tables as if she might contract acute viral meningitis or be forced to vote Democratic by so doing. Instead, she had spent virtually all of her time at Old Bunbury regaling anyone and everyone within earshot about the myriad details of her most recent New Zealand escapades. Most listened with a dutiful, reluctant, and sympathetic patience, primarily in deference to the two harrowing encounters Esther had experienced with the club's now-disgraced former member and internationally wanted escaped murderer. Following the good advice of both President Clive and Detective Giztips, Esther had judiciously avoided talking about Hamish P. Tumorington with anyone other than the police and the club's Board of Directors, even though more than a few members and staff were luridly curious and unceasingly persistent with their questions in this regard.

Apparently, today's corner four-top of Clive Endive "Clive-man" Ogive IV, J. Eaton "Eat-o" Swank, Art "Check My Pulse" Le Fever, and Danny "Tuxedo Man" Bumbery was to Esther's liking, because on this cloudless, lower-than-normal-humidity, 78-degree Fahrenheit (25.55 degrees Celsius) early Tuesday afternoon, Esther, after marching through the front door of the club like she owned the place, approached their table in an unusually briskly paced and cheery-eyed manner.

"Good afternoon, gentlemen," Esther bubbled. Esther being friendlier than usual was *always* cause for guarded concern on the part of anyone and everyone who knew her well. "I think I will do you four distinguished gentlemen the distinct honor of taking your lunch orders this perfect early fall day."

"Hello, Esther," answered a cautious Clive for the fearsome foursome. "Thank you for your most kind and generous offer, but I believe that Poinsettia Derswoggle has already been assigned to wait on us."

"No problem, boss. I'll just tell that well-meaning but prissy stuff-shirt that I will handle things from here on out. Yes, good old Mrs. Derswoggle has been at Old Bunbury longer than most all of the other wait staff—not nearly as long as I, of course—but she could still learn a thing or two about professional service. To be fair, I've seen worse waitresses in my time. Poinsettia, at least, is always willing to give it the old college try."

"Clive was just telling us about all your latest adventures in New Zealand," said Eat-o, deftly changing the subject. He was smart enough to recognize a no-win situation when he saw one. Plus, waitress assignment was clearly an operational issue, and, internationally acclaimed private club savant that he was, Eat-o knew far better than most that board members should *always* and *only* concern themselves with governance matters. *Good luck with this one, Jay!* "First off, I want to extend my personal congratulations on your being made an honorary lifetime member of the prestigious and exclusive Kaikoura Whaling & Sailing Club! That's quite an honor, Esther!"

"Thank you very much, Mr. Swank," said Esther, the swelling pride obvious in both her bodily demeanor and tone of voice. "It was totally unexpected, I can assure you. The longtime president of the club, Rutherford Sparnacle—I know you remember him from the Old Bunbury Member Guest of several years ago—was incredibly gracious the entire time I was in Kaikoura. I certainly hope to see him again real soon."

"I suspect you will, Esther," said Clive agreeably. "I will surely be having Rusty back to our club one of these days. Anything new from Detective Giztips?" he asked, purposely sending the conversation into another direction.

"Not a thing, boss. As far as the police are concerned, Mr. Tumorington may as well have fallen off the face of the earth. No one knows if he has even returned to the United States. Perhaps he has decided that his best chance for continuing freedom is to keep away from this part of the world altogether."

"Perhaps, Esther," piped in a dubious Tuxedo Man, "but I wouldn't count on it. Hamish P. Tumorington was always one pretty weird dude, as far as I am concerned. There were more than a few times when I thought the man was playing with fifty or fifty-one cards, tops. I know he had, and presumably still has, impeccable taste when it comes to private club pillow selection, arrangement, repairs, and maintenance—an extremely rare and highly desirable skill set that deserves every great private club member's enthusiastic support and unending admiration—but I also remember him to be one *very* serious-minded, high-strung, and fiercely determined person. If he specifically told you that he was going to exact lethal revenge, I would take him at his word."

"As would I," agreed a somber Dr. Art Le Fever. "I suggest that you be on your guard at *all* times, Esther, at least for the foreseeable future. Let's just hope that the police get a break as to Hamish's whereabouts sooner rather than later and put that heinous murderer and abject disgrace to Old Bunbury back in jail."

"Sound advice all around, Esther," said Clive for the group. "Now, if you are not otherwise occupied, would you be kind enough to take our lunch orders?"

"Of course, gentlemen. There is no need for any of you to say an additional word. As you surely know, I am fully aware of *all* of your lunchtime favorites and will immediately proceed to the kitchen to place the orders. Dr. Le Fever," she added, looking directly at Art, "since it is apparent to all of us how well you have been doing of late with your persistent 'weight-management challenges,' please consider this your lucky day. You chili dog smothered in onions with two ice-cold Heinekens will be coming up shortly," said Esther amicably as she left their four-top for the kitchen's swinging door.

"Let's hope she actually makes it to the kitchen without getting sidetracked to regale some unsuspecting members or otherwise-occupied employees with unasked-for details about her latest New Zealand escapades," said Clive when Esther was out of earshot, verbalizing what the entire table was thinking.

After a few moments of comfortable silence, Eat-o said quietly to his tablemates, "I'm really worried about her, men. She is putting up a good front, but even Esther, in her heart of hearts, has to be concerned. When someone as wealthy, connected, and determined as Hamish P. Tumorington threatens lethal revenge, you have to take what the man says seriously."

"I agree," echoed Danny. "We haven't heard the last of this."

"Let's just hope she heeds the excellent advice of Adam Giztips and doesn't try to solve the case all by herself. The four us know better than most that Esther gives new meaning to independent and feisty," said Clive.

"Amen," muttered the other three tablemates simultaneously, as if they were affirming a statement of epic religious proportions.

"Hey, has anyone given any thought to this afternoon's game of golf?" asked Art, once again moving the conversation away from Esther. "Whoever gets the Clive-man for a partner is going to be in deep trouble. I don't want him on my team, that's for sure. He's been on the golf struggle-bus of late."

"I'll take my chances with him," said Eat-o in a brave gesture of noble camaraderie. "History shows that the Clive-man can raise his game to another level when the chips are on the table."

"Thanks, Eat-o," said Clive gratefully to his longtime great friend. "The grass may be greener on the other side of the fence, Art, but it may prove more difficult to mow."

"Then it's settled. Eat-o and the Clive-man versus Check My Pulse and me," said Tuxedo Man resolutely, fending off any additional discussion or potential dispute.

Soon thereafter, Esther arrived at their table and set down everyone's orders. To the foursome's collective astonishment, the correct orders had been presented—and in a timely manner, to boot.

"Will wonders never cease," said Clive amicably.

"Have a good lunch and game of golf, gentlemen," said Esther, ignoring Clive's good-natured barb. Sensing that the group had official club business to discuss, Esther promptly wandered off to do whatever it was that she thought she had to do next.

"Before we tee it up, gentlemen, as president of this most distinguished club, I need your sound and confidential board member advice on one small point of business," said Clive quietly to the group. "It seems that we have a new member who apparently wants to file a grievance with the Board of Directors because we won't put him on the Grievance Committee. Any suggestions?"

"Yes," said Eat-o emphatically. "Just remind this new member—I'll be kind and not mention his name, even though we all know full well about whom we are speaking—that *great* private clubs like Old Bunbury neither have nor require Grievance Committees. Never had and never will. Tell him that if he keeps this nonsense up, the Board of Directors will immediately revoke his Old Bunbury membership—family connections be damned—and he can then spend *all* his time at the second-tier club in Southeast Florida to which he also belongs, proudly serving on *their* inane Grievance Committee. If *any* private club needs a Grievance Committee, it's surely that one. Now, let's finish our lunches and go play some golf."

Derwood Entwhistle is having considerable difficulty understanding why Old Bunbury has never had, and will never have, a Grievance Committee.

Chapter 24

Final Preparations

Hamish had spent the previous twenty-four hours, save for a calculated run to a Walmart Supercenter forty-five miles away to pick up a few last-minute supplies, holed up at Steele's Family Motel & RV Park meticulously preparing for the denouement of his master plan of revenge. The shabby lodging establishment on the once bustling but now largely ramshackle four-lane highway he had found on the internet was certainly appropriately inconspicuous and suitably located for his purposes, but that was not the primary reason why it had first caught his inquisitive eye; Hamish thought the *name* of the squalid excuse for a place to spend the night was perfect, just perfect.

Hamish had gone over the details of his cleverly constructed plan again and again, and he was now fully confident that he had systematically thought through every possible detail and readied himself for all potential contingencies. Mr. Rich V. Steele was now more than eager to proceed, although he knew full well that once the final act was set in motion, there would be no turning back.

All things considered, Hamish believed that he was adequately prepared to start his new life when the final act of his dastardly play had been successfully completed. Yes, he might have done still better in this regard, given more time, thought, and effort, but he nonetheless congratulated himself on all that he had so far accomplished. As but one example, Hamish's extensive research had told him that eighty-four countries around the world had specifically chosen not to enact extradition treaties of any sort with the United States. In effect, these were countries that purposely wanted to tie the hands of United States law-enforcement officials, most likely for political or philosophical reasons, if and when such law-enforcement officials ever attempted to return a felonious citizen to sovereign American soil. Hamish's just-completed visit to Dubai had confirmed in person what he had already concluded in theory: The United Arab Emirates, in his considered opinion the most desirable of the eighty-four candidates, would be the ideal place for him to call his new home. In Dubai, sophisticated, cosmopolitan, vibrant city-state that it was, mega-wealthy westerners were as common as illegal aliens in the United States casting ill-informed, illicit presidential ballots for Barack Hussein Obama. There, he could and would live, with complete confidence and total anonymity, the privileged life of luxury that he had heretofore always enjoyed—save for his entirely forgettable and all-too-long detour to the United States federal prison system.

To properly prepare for his new life, Mr. Rich V. Steele had also done, although sometimes with great reluctance, other things he knew were required if he were to successfully move forward. For example, he had gradually eliminated all bank and credit card information in the name of Hamish P. Tumorington. As painful as it had been, Hamish had also instructed his financial team to dispose of all his United States real estate holdings. (He would, at least for now, retain his luxury properties in Europe, South America, and the Far East.) The timing, from a financial point of view, could not have been much worse; nearly everything had gone for a significant loss. His spectacular three-bedroom ski chalet in Angel Fire, New Mexico; his custom-designed, lushly landscaped estate in Bonita Springs, Florida; his rustic oceanfront cottage in Seabrook, Washington; and his turnkey mountain retreat in Blowing Rock, North Carolina, were now nothing more than fond memories. Alas! He had even forced himself to sell his long-owned nine-bedroom, one-hundred-seven-year-old mansion not all that far from Old Bunbury, the only property that (thankfully!) had gone for a tidy profit.

Hamish had done other things as well to ease the transition to his new life. He had, for example, changed his appearance in a number of ways and would continue to do so further once he was settled in Dubai. He was already sporting clothes in a style radically different from the Hamish P. Tumorington of old, as well as wearing contact lenses that made his sandy brown irises appear cerulean blue. *I look pretty cool as a blue-eyed dude!* Perhaps when he got to Dubai, he would also alter the color and style of his hair and maybe even grow a handlebar moustache, a facial accoutrement that had always intrigued him. Who knows, he might even use his wealth and connections to locate a talented and discreet cosmetic surgeon who could and would, for the right sum of money, make appropriate changes to the shape of his aquiline nose and craggy, handsome chin. Hamish P. Tumorington, aka Rich V. Steele, had done and would continue to do everything he could to bury his old identity and forge a new one. Few had ever done more in this regard—except, of course, one Barack Hussein Obama, the nefarious and despicable American president who, while campaigning on "open government" and "full disclosure," had sealed his birth records, passport records, medical records, grade-school and high-school records from Hawaii's snooty Punahou School, undergraduate records from Occidental College (including the recently discovered and incontrovertible fact that he attended there on a scholarship reserved *exclusively* for foreign-born students), undergraduate records (including his thesis) from Columbia University, records from Harvard Law School, and legislative records from the Illinois State Senate. *Other than that, good old Obama's life is an open book! America,* what *in the world were you thinking?*

Hamish had done still other things to properly prepare for what lay ahead. For example, over the course of the past few years, he had gradually transferred the bulk of his financial assets to banks based in George Town in the Cayman

Islands; Buenos Aires, Argentina; and Geneva, Switzerland. Now that he had officially chosen the United Arab Emirates as his new home, he could and would begin transferring additional wealth there as well. He had also, over time, cut personal ties with everyone save a very few close business confidants, lifelong personal friends, and selected members of his immediate family, all people who would take to their grave anything and everything they knew about him.

While at the Walmart Supercenter—one purposely chosen so far away so as to effectively eliminate his chances of being recognized—Hamish had purchased three roles of silver duct tape, twenty-five feet of nylon rope, assorted junk foods to consume over the course of his secretive stay at Steele's Family Motel & RV Park, and, most importantly, ammunition for the handgun that one of his toadies had surreptitiously obtained for him in an off-the-books cash transaction with a shady street dealer. Not that it mattered—Hamish didn't know or care a lick about guns and, except for the necessity of what he was about to do, preferred to keep it that way—but the weapon was an unregistered and untraceable Smith & Wesson .38-caliber pistol, the weapon of choice for those who preferred the most state-of-the-art, concealable, and accurate personal protection possible. It obviously could and would do "the job." Obtaining the illegal gun, Hamish had subsequently learned, had been easier than getting a Democrat to vote more than once in United States presidential elections.

Sitting on the frayed and faded purple-striped bedspread covering the sagging, lumpy mattress, Hamish once again surveyed his decrepit surroundings. In no more than a week, if all went according to plan, he would have successfully completed his business with that self-righteous busybody who, for reasons unfathomable to any sane person, had somehow fashioned herself an expert private-club waitress. If all went well, he also would have triumphantly settled into his new life in the astonishing, endless-possibilities city-state of Dubai. There would be no need to stay in a hovel like this *ever* again.

Yes, all was ready. The supplies required to complete his forthcoming work filled the leather satchel at his feet. His pistol was sitting on the nearby undusted dresser, a weapon he had checked so many times to make sure it was fully loaded that there was no need to ever look again.

It was time to begin the final act of his macabre play.

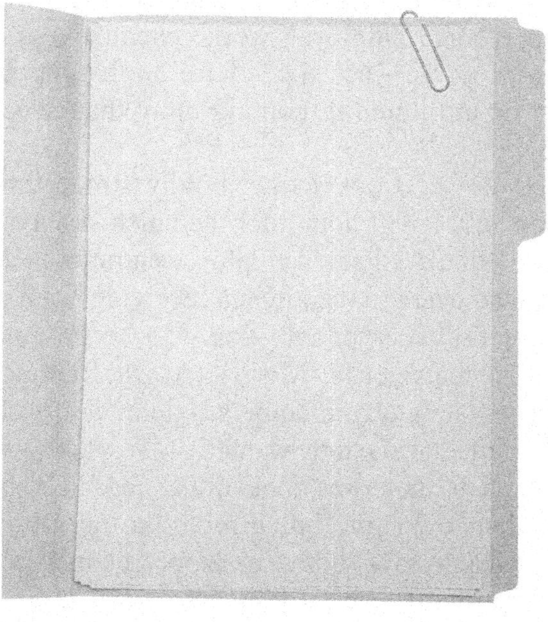

This manila folder contains everything the American people know for certain about the background of Barack Hussein Obama as well as all that he did to prevent the brutal murder of United States citizens in Benghazi.

Chapter 25

Missing

Esther next returned to Old Bunbury on Thursday around eleven thirty in the morning for a lunchtime shift that, faith and begorrah, she was actually scheduled to work. Because she rarely, if ever, visited the small but comfortably appointed employee break room in the clubhouse basement—the location of the bulletin board where the weekly food and beverage employee work schedule was regularly posted for all to see—her appearance on this particular day could best be attributed to nothing more than sheer coincidence.

As was her wont, Esther boldly strode through the front door nearly a half hour after the lunch service had officially begun—the designated employee entrance at the rear of the building adjacent to the kitchen receiving dock was obviously meant for *other* people—only to be promptly intercepted by club manager Jay Morris. (At Old Bunbury, like all truly great private clubs, members ordered and were served *what* they wanted, *when* they wanted, *where* they wanted, and *how* they wanted; there was none of that nonsense about closing the kitchen and main dining room during certain slower times of the day to save money on labor. If a member wanted well-done scrambled eggs with extra jalapeños, a triple-decker club sandwich on toasted pumpernickel minus the typically accompanying Mrs. Alfredo's traditional kosher dill pickle, or medium-rare chateaubriand with herb roasted new potatoes and Béarnaise sauce, he or she could and would have it, no matter if it were nine in the morning or nine at night; the logoed, embossed menus were no more than a list of suggestions rarely utilized by the members or something with which to impress the occasional guest.)

"Hello, Esther. It's good to see that you are actually adhering to the posted work schedule," deadpanned Jay.

"Yes, it is," Esther answered cordially, clueless as to whether the best club manager for whom she had ever worked was joshing or not. "What can I do for you?"

"I need your advice and help," he said in a tone noticeably more solemn and officious than typical. "Please follow me to my office."

"Certainly, Jay," Esther replied, the bonhomie gone from her voice. It was clear that Jay was truly worried about something.

After they had both entered Jay's office and taken their respective seats, Jay said without preamble, "As you surely know, the club's Pillow Committee had their regular fortnightly meeting last evening. It is a crucially important time for this esteemed group, as they are down to the final eight pillow designs and accompanying color palettes. Their final selection will be an essential part of the long-anticipated and much-needed remodeling of Old Bunbury's storied Reading Room. I must tell you that everyone, especially Chairwoman Ruth McFarland Whitestone, was completely taken aback by the fact that President Clive was not in attendance. So I have to ask, Esther: Do *you* have any clue as to why he excused himself from last evening's gathering?"

"Yes, Jay, I did hear that the President Clive failed to show. While we both know that our beloved leader does not attend every single club committee meeting—if he did, he would have absolutely no life whatsoever outside of Old Bunbury—I agree that it is highly unlikely for him to miss one so critical to the very long-term social and financial viability of our great club. I was going to ask you the very same question after today's lunch rush."

"It's good to see that you and I are on the same page," said a slightly relieved Jay. "As far as I can tell, no one has seen President Clive since he drove home late Tuesday afternoon after his stellar round of golf. I also know that he failed to show for yesterday's scheduled lunch and eighteen holes. Dr. Le Fever and Mr. Bumbery were eagerly looking forward to a rematch after getting so thoroughly trounced by President Clive and Mr. Swank earlier in the week. Apparently, Old Bunbury's big kahuna is on a tear with his new Titleist Cameron California Sea Mist Fastback Putter and Taylormade R7 CGB MAX Limited Driver."

"I'll tell you what," said Esther, whose grave tone of voice and resolute demeanor were not dissimilar to Jay's, "let me look into the matter further and see what I can find out. This whole situation feels wrong, very wrong, to me."

"I agree, Esther. Thank you, as always, for your concern and help. Please let me know what you discover."

For the next two hours, Esther, sitting alone in the dark, narrow alcove off the club's historic, soon-to-be-remodeled Reading Room, called anyone and everyone whom she thought might be able to help. She began by speaking with Old Bunbury's beloved club president's only son, Clive Endive Ogive V. "Clive Five," as he was known to virtually everyone, both in and out of the club, was a junior member who rarely made use of his highly coveted legacy membership, a birthright that he had officially inherited as a wonderful surprise on his eighteenth birthday. Clive Five was currently in his third year at Yale Law School and doing exceptionally well. He told Esther that it was very nice to speak with her but that he hadn't heard from his father in nearly two weeks, their last conversation being when he had called from Cape Kidnappers to gush about the spectacular beauty of the famed New Zealand golf course that he and his good buddy Rusty Sparnacle had just played. (The Clive-man and Clive Five, who had had the typical tumultuous father-son relationship during the son's rebellious teenage years, had once again grown close after Clive Five had subsequently "found himself" and hunkered down to his legal studies.)

Esther next spoke with her boss's only other child, Buffy Flannery Ogive. She was also now on very close terms with her father after having not spoken with him for the three years immediately following Clive's brutal divorce from his first wife—Buffy's mother—Millicent Victoria (nee Rockefeller) Ogive. The anger and bitterness between Millicent and Clive during that ugly, forgettable period in the Ogive family had long since dissipated. The two of them, in fact, had actually become far more accepting of each other's foibles as platonic friends and social acquaintances over the past decade than they had ever been as husband and wife; they were, in fact, occasionally seen chatting together happily both at important, "mandatory-attendance" societal foofoos and at celebrations of family milestones.

Like her older brother, Buffy had sown more than her fair share of wild oats during her frenetic undergraduate years. And, like Clive Five, she had also outgrown her youthful rambunctious nature and matured to the point where she was now a highly attractive and eligible young lady as well as an honors student in biomimetics at the prestigious Radcliffe Institute for Advanced Study at Harvard.

During their conversation, Buffy told Esther that she had last spoken with her father about ten days prior. She also expressed her surprise and concern that her father had suddenly gone absent from Old Bunbury apparently without telling anyone, especially during such a busy time of year. Buffy then sincerely thanked Esther for her call—it had been far too long, she rued, since the two lifetime acquaintances had last spoken. Buffy concluded their conversation by making Esther promise that Esther would call her back *immediately* when she had found something out.

Esther's next triumvirate of calls was to Clive's three ex-wives. Although Millicent was quite concerned and offered to help in any way she could, neither of the other two were particularly talkative or helpful. More accurately, both expressed minimal interest in the fact that that their former spouse seemed to have gone suddenly and inexplicably missing. Clive's second wife, the snooty socialite and über-wealthy heiress Madison MacLaine (nee Brennan) Ogive, in fact, had actually snorted a huffy "Good riddance!" before abruptly hanging up. Clive's third wife, Clemencia Tabatha (nee Snerdly) Ogive—a union that nearly everyone had (correctly) predicted would not last more than six months—had been only slightly less rude. "Clem the Gem," as the Old Bunbury oldsters had sarcastically nicknamed Clemencia, may have had (in her prime) a Lamborghini for an exterior, but it had always been powered by the engine of a Chevrolet Volt.

Esther's final call was to Clive's current girlfriend, Adelaide Lilith Thistlecatcher, a stunningly attractive and ungodly wealthy woman a full three decades younger than Clive—and someone whom Esther had met only twice. Adelaide and Clive, Esther knew, were not romantically involved though were not averse to the occasional sweaty, clandestine, noncommittal roll in the hay when and as circumstances permitted. (Clive was, Esther knew, getting the preponderance of *that* particular aspect of his life fulfilled with his fortnightly visits to the Miss Kitty's Happy Dragon Asian Day Spa & Aromatherapy Parlor in the adjacent township—but that was a topic for another day.) No, Clive and Adelaide accompanied each other to those social occasions where going alone would have been noticeably awkward, an arrangement that, at least for the time being, had proven satisfactory for the both of them. Adelaide, to Esther's great dismay, told Esther that had not seen or spoken with Clive in nearly three weeks.

When Esther had exhausted all the obvious possibilities, she hurried back to the manager's office. "No luck, Jay," she told him, skipping the preliminaries. "I have spoken with everyone I could think of. I even considered calling Consuela Gimpelstein, Clive's longtime housekeeper, until I realized she would almost certainly not be of any help."

"Gimpelstein? I thought her last name was Fernandez," said a confused Jay.

"Remember, Jay, she got married four months ago. Since that time, she has only worked part time—Mondays and Fridays, to be exact—so literally dozens of people have seen and spoken with President Clive since Consuela and the big boss were last together. However, in the interest of leaving absolutely no stone unturned, I will give her a call, probably tomorrow morning, if nothing else turns up."

"Makes sense," agreed Jay.

"Like you, Jay, I am starting to get worried, very worried indeed," Esther concluded. "It is not at all like President Clive to go completely off campus without letting at least *someone* know. Typically, when it comes to Old Bunbury, it is either you or I."

"I agree," answered Jay pensively. "Tell you what, Esther. Why don't you take the rest of the day off, go home, and keep working on trying to find out something. We both know that you know more about all things Old Bunbury than anyone else on the planet. If you come up with anything, anything at all, please let me know immediately. I am going to call Adam Giztips and share our mutual concern with the good detective. I know that he will do everything in his power to help out as well."

"Fair enough, Jay," said Esther. "Let's stay in close touch on this."

Socialite Adelaide Lilith Thistlecatcher enjoys the occasional furtive and sweaty roll in the hay with the Clive-man.

Chapter 26

Trapped

Clive Endive Ogive IV was reasonably sure that he had opened his eyes, but he could not be certain. He believed that he had just felt both his eyelids break contact with the puffy, slightly moist skin directly below his eye sockets and flick instantly upwards—an action that the body's autonomic nervous system typically handled without one's conscious control or sensation—but perhaps the whole thing had been nothing more than some sort of cruel deception. Taking another breath, Clive purposely re-closed his eyelids and slowly, intentionally repeated the same simplistic movement of re-opening them. Yes, he was now convinced that his eyes were indeed wide open but either it was pitch black wherever he was or he had suddenly and inexplicably gone blind.

No, not true, he thought after a seeming eternity had elapsed. There, through a small barred and cracked window high above his vantage point, oozed the faintest of faint hints of grayish light. He was neither blind nor losing his mind. *I need to stand up and explore my surroundings.*

But, of course, Clive could not stand. In that instant, the horrible circumstances of his dire situation came flooding back. He first remembered that he had been drifting in and out of consciousness for a fairly long time, reasonably certain that his current state of heavy, unnatural stupor was drug-induced, but he was baffled as to the specifics. He had no way of knowing where he was or how long he had been here, wherever here was, but the pervasive soreness of his muscles—the combined result, no doubt, of the contorted, semi-recumbent position in which he now found himself and the previous periodic exertion of attempting to free himself—as well as the bursting fullness of his overinflated bladder told him that at least twelve hours, and perhaps significantly more time, had already passed.

Clive, now fully alert, took careful stock of his current predicament. His raw and bloody wrists were bound tightly, uncomfortably so, behind his back with some sort of thick rope and what felt like ordinary duct tape. His ankles, firmly lashed together as well, were also tightly affixed to a thick metal rod protruding from the bottom of the wall of the dank, claustrophobia-inducing building that now held him hostage. His parched mouth was completely stuffed with a bitter-tasting cloth firmly secured in place by still more duct tape wrapped multiple times around his aching skull. Though he could breathe well enough through his unblocked nasal passages, the material filling his mouth prevented him from making any sound louder than a pathetic, muffled whimper. Though he did not yet know the details, Clive was certain that the horrible situation he now found himself in was a result of the dastardly work of one Hamish P. Tumorington.

Thinking through the sequence of events from the previous two days, Clive clearly remembered leaving Old Bunbury late Tuesday afternoon after he and Eat-o had thoroughly trounced Check My Pulse and Tuxedo Man in their regular golf match. He had really been on his game, smoothing his drives further than he had in the past decade, more often than not to the dead centers of Old Bunbury's narrow, immaculately maintained, tightly bunkered fairways. He had been equally exceptional on the greens, three-putting only once and never missing from inside five feet. He and Eat-o had won handily five and four, and the match had really never been that close.

Following a quick adult libation with the boys at the club—Check My Pulse and Tuxedo Man had been gracious in defeat but had made Clive and Eat-o commit to a rematch the following day—Clive had left the club and gone straight home. He had located, nuked, and stomached, with marginal interest, what his longtime housekeeper, Consuela, had prepared and left for him in the pantry refrigerator before she had gone home late Monday afternoon—it might have been some concoction of minced, over-salted gefilte fish balls topped with bland sliced boiled carrots and lumpy horseradish sauce—and washed it down, far more enthusiastically, with two double-vodka gimlets. (Consuela, who had never been much of a cook, had gone off the culinary deep end after her recent marriage to the wealthy local banker Mort Gimpelstein. If Clive had thought Consuela's cheese and onion enchiladas were bad—and she was Mexican by birth and the daughter of a celebrated chef—he had known nothing until he had to consume her frightening attempts at "cooking Jewish"! Clive, however, had resigned himself to the fact that he would, at least for the foreseeable future, remain a gentleman and continue to act as the gustatory Guinea pig for his loyal and hardworking housekeeper of twenty-nine years. Besides, he was lucky to still have her in his employ at all; her recent nuptials had made her a very wealthy woman.)

After dinner, Clive had played fetch with his chocolate Labrador, Lucy, for almost an hour—she was by far the most ball-obsessed dog he had ever known—and, following that, had given a quick once-over to the fifty-seven unopened e-mails cluttering his in-box. There had been nothing, he recalled, so pressing that an appropriate response couldn't wait until the following morning. After washing up and donning his toffee-colored charmeuse pajamas, Clive had settled into his comfortable authentic nineteenth-century mahogany barrel-back chair in the spacious den directly across from his oversized wood-burning fireplace and enjoyed the next few chapters of Greg Iles's *The Quiet Game,* the first novel in which the salty but lovable protagonist Penn Cage made an appearance. (Clive had recently discovered the wonderfully captivating and evocative novels of Greg Iles and was currently happily engrossed in the process of devouring each and every one of them.) It hadn't been long before Clive had drifted off to a deep and dreamless sleep. And that was the last thing he remembered—until he woke up confused and shivering in this dark, dank unknown hell-hole, unceremoniously hog-tied, unable to free himself, and, truth be told, eerily frightened of what might next occur.

Clive had no semblance of an idea as to what to do next. He took a closer look around the dimly lit building and saw that it was filled with assorted, mostly rusted, pipes, gauges, pumps, and valves of various sizes and shapes. The concrete-slab floor was covered with a choke-inducing combination of the powdered remnants of what had once been tree leaves, a thick layer of dust, and the occasional scrap of yellowing notebook paper. Not in the least mechanically inclined, Clive was therefore unable to deduce anything specific about either the building's possible uses or likely whereabouts with any degree of accuracy. It was obvious that he could not break free from his restraints; his bloodied wrists and aching, cramping muscles were proof enough that his previous semiconscious attempts at so doing had been thoroughly unsuccessful. Although Clive repeatedly told himself not to yield to the insipient fear and surging panic that seemed to be surreptitiously overtaking his entire being, he could feel himself gradually losing the battle. Could he ever get out of here? Would he ever escape?

Lost in his jumbled thoughts and atavistic fears, Clive was abruptly startled to see the door at the other end of the room creak open. The silhouette that entered through the accompanying swirling cloud of dust and debris quickly closed the door behind him and strode purposefully towards where Clive lay.

"Hello, Clive," said the soft, near-effeminate voice of the person whom Clive had known in his heart of hearts that his unwelcome visitor would be. Clive's fervent hopes for a miraculous savior had obviously been for naught.

"What's that?" joked a fiendish Hamish P. Tumorington. "Cat's got your tongue? Alas, it is indeed most unfortunate that you are unable to converse. I see that you have somehow gotten yourself into what appears to be a most undesirable predicament, hands and feet securely bound and mouth stuffed so full that you cannot utter more than a muted, indiscernible grunt. Given that this is the case, I will be kind enough to do the talking for the both of us. I suspect that I already have an excellent idea as to what sorts of questions might be running through your obviously confused, angry, and scared mind, so please allow me the distinct pleasure and honor of now satisfying your curiosity.

"You are currently being held captive in the old and long-abandoned Old Bunbury golf course irrigation pump house in the dense woods not all that far from the fourteenth green. No one, other than you and I, has entered this building for at least two decades. I would hazard to guess that the majority of today's club members are unaware that this decrepit, long-forgotten excuse for a building even exists. You and I do, of course, because, as you will recall, we proudly served together on the Grounds Committee the year the replacement irrigation system for the golf course was installed and the accompanying new stone block pump house between the fifth green and the sixth tee constructed. That was, I am proud to say, the very first Old Bunbury club committee on which I had the honor and privilege to serve. It was no Pillow Committee, of course, when it comes to the world of private club glory and prestige, but it was, I must admit, a decent-enough start to my long and distinguished committee career. You are presently, I am delighted to point out, a paradigm example of someone who is being hidden in plain sight."

Seeing that he had captured Clive's full and undivided attention, Hamish pressed on with fiendish delight. "I have returned to Old Bunbury this one final time, as by now you surely have deduced, to exact my revenge on both you, the club president who oversaw, sanctioned, and even encouraged my unceremonious expulsion from the club, and Esther, that insolent, know-it-all, miserable excuse for a waitress who successfully identified me as the vicious murderer of Alfie Johnson—someone, I might add, who thoroughly deserved everything he got. I would also note that if it weren't for that untalented reprobate, I would now be serving on, and perhaps even chairing, the ultra-exclusive, internationally acclaimed Old Bunbury Pillow Committee. But alas, none of us can alter the past, no matter how much we may rue the day.

"To be perfectly candid, neither you nor Esther will survive the next twelve hours. By the time your rotting, fetid bodies are discovered and identified, I will have successfully left the country and settled into my new life of unbridled wealth, uninterrupted leisure, and sybaritic pleasure.

"Clive, you are, if nothing else, a man who truly understands and enthusiastically savors life's subtle pleasures," Hamish continued, now on a gleeful, demonic roll, "so I know you can appreciate the special irony of your spending your final hours in a building that sits less than two hundred feet from the spot where the brutalized body of Alfie Johnson was discovered. My plan for revenge is really quite simple: After we finish our one-sided conversation and I take my leave of this godforsaken structure, I am going to call Esther on *your* cell phone—yes, I have your soon-to-be-a-relic Blackberry Bold right here in my new, regular-fit Wrangler jeans' left front pocket—and tell her that if she ever hopes to save your miserable, pathetic life, she will meet me tonight—*alone*—directly outside this building precisely at midnight. Esther, of course, knows full well both the existence and location of this dilapidated structure. She will be made to understand in no uncertain terms that if she informs anyone else about our conversation—and I do mean *anyone*—your life will be terminated immediately and in a most painful manner.

For reasons well beyond my ability to comprehend, Esther absolutely worships the very ground upon which you tread, so I am quite confident that she will fully comply with my simple instructions. You will discover the remaining gory details of the final act of my macabre play after Esther arrives.

"One more thing," added a now overtly gloating Hamish, the irrational, demented glare in his eyes apparent to Clive even in the eerie dimness of the room, "I know you are wondering exactly how you ended up in Old Bunbury's long-abandoned pump house. It is actually quite simple. I easily broke into your house yesterday afternoon when you were playing golf at the club—congratulations, by the way, on such a stellar round—and waited quietly in the large closet in what was Clive Five's bedroom of his youth. Once I was certain that you had fallen fast asleep, I simply crept down the stairs, snuck up behind you, and injected you with an appropriate dose of propofol. As you may or may not be aware, propofol is the short-acting hypnotic agent currently favored by general anesthesiologists in thousands of hospitals in more than fifty countries around the world. It is, in effect, the modern version of sodium thiopental—and, in case you are curious, is currently being marketed quite successfully by AstraZeneca under the trade name Diprivan. The drug obviously works "as advertised" because, if you woke up at all from the unsuspecting jab of my syringe, it was only for a few short seconds. After that, it was merely a matter of loading you into my car, making the short drive to the isolated employee parking area here at the club—a space that, coincidentally, is not all that far from this very abandoned pump house—and toting you to our current location. The fact that you are relatively small in stature and have retained your youthful slim physique made transporting your unconscious body not all that difficult. The duct tape and ropes that now prevent you from standing, talking, and escaping are of the ordinary, everyday Walmart Supercenter variety. I think we can both agree that they have proven quite effective in their current application. And, as they say, 'the rest is history,'" boasted Hamish with devilish delight, finally concluding his lengthy monologue of pre-meditated revenge.

"Before I take my leave, Clive, I want you to understand and appreciate that I am behaving in a perfectly logical manner and simply doing what needs to be done. I truly believe that a prison life with little, if any, chance of parole would have ultimately driven me mad. Accordingly, when the appropriate opportunity presented itself, I had no other choice but to escape. I will never go back to jail again—*never*—for as long as I am able walk on our good planet Earth. That aside, you and Esther must surely atone for the grave and unforgivable sins of enthusiastically conspiring with the police to identify, arrest, and incarcerate me. Indeed, you both will soon be making the ultimate sacrifice and joining the everlasting oblivion of humanity's billions who have already begun their permanent dirt naps."

With that, Hamish reached deftly into the right front pocket of his jeans and removed a menacing-looking syringe filled with what Clive (correctly) assumed to be Diprivan. Clive's eyes grew wide with primeval terror as, like a fresh-out-of-the-water fish, he flailed helplessly in a futile attempt at escape. Clive knew he could do nothing, nothing at all, to prevent what was about to happen.

"Relax, Clive-man," said Hamish in a tone that would have made Marcus Welby sound uncaring. "I want you to understand that I am not a total monster—yet. This additional shot of propofol, I can assure you, will not be fatal; rather, like the doses I have previously administered to you, it will help your next few hours pass more quickly and comfortably. Consider it a last personal favor from one former Old Bunbury member to one current Old Bunbury president. Esther and I will see you not all that long after you have reawoken. Sleep tight."

A few of the rusty pipes lining the walls of the long-abandoned Old Bunbury golf course irrigation pump house.

Chapter 27

Eureka!

As the day wore on, Esther became increasingly convinced that Old Bunbury's longtime and highly revered president was in very serious, and likely grave, danger. Although Esther did not yet know the specifics, her uncannily accurate—more than a few would say infallible—gut feelings when it came to all things Old Bunbury told her in no uncertain terms that President Clive's absence was the direct and indisputable result of Hamish P. Tumorington's presence. Esther realized that she had to combine her encyclopedic knowledge of the club with her long-established, well-honed powers of deduction and near-clairvoyant intuition to discover the locations of both President Clive and Mr. Tumorington before it was too late. Equally as important, Esther knew she had to work *fast*.

Taking steady, purposefully deep breaths to calm herself, Esther carefully pored yet again over the myriad details of her many telephone calls from earlier in the day. Everyone she had spoken with had expressed genuine sympathy and frank concern about President Clive's whereabouts—except, of course, for his second and third ex-wives. The more Esther recollected their exact words as well as the manner in which the ex-wives had spoken, the more she assessed the attitudes of Madison MacLaine (nee Brennan) Ogive and Clemencia Tabatha (nee Snerdly) Ogive as something beyond mere indifference and a lack of cooperation; it was more accurate to say that they had been openly hostile. Neither big-haired, gold-digging bimbo had ever much cared for Esther—a feeling, she was not averse to admitting, that had been mutual. Esther had always known that they disliked and distrusted her precisely because she recognized them both for the shallow, social-climbing floozies they were—and they knew that she knew. Were their current outright antagonistic attitudes merely the result of a lingering animosity that can and does occur between spouses when marriages do not end well, or were they something more? Could Caddy Maddie or Clem the Gem actually have had something to do with President Clive's sudden and inexplicable disappearance? Worse, could one or both of them somehow be in malevolent cahoots with Hamish P. Tumorington in some grandiose plot of universal revenge?

Esther was startled back to the present by the soothingly familiar ringtone of her iPhone 5: the dulcet yet powerful voice of Sammy Davis Jr. belting out "I've Gotta Be Me." (If there *ever* was a song whose lyrics were custom-made for Esther, this was it.) A quick glance at the screen confirmed that it was President Clive's private number. Finally!

"Hello, Esther. This is Hamish P. Tumorington," whispered the sinister, eerie voice on the other end of the line.

"Mr. Tumorington! Why are you calling me on President Clive's cell phone? How did you get it? Where are you? Is my boss alright?" she rambled, the incipient fear causing her voice to crackle unnaturally.

"Please listen carefully, Esther," came the calm and controlled reply, completely ignoring her rapid-fire litany of frantic questions. "I am going to say what I have to say only once. It is now Thursday late afternoon, and I know that you are back home after a purposely truncated visit to Old Bunbury. I also know that you, Jay Morris, and Detective Giztips, each in your own way, are now feverishly attempting to find out why your beloved Clive Endive Ogive IV has suddenly and unexplainably gone missing and, more importantly, just where he might be. The good news is that I am going to tell you, and *only* you, the answers to both of these life-changing questions on one, and only one, simple condition: that you do not tell anyone about this conversation. Not that mediocre, ass-kissing excuse for a private club manager, Jay Morris. Not the meddlesome, overly officious Detective Adam Giztips. Not *anyone.* If you do, your beloved Clive Endive Ogive IV will experience an immediate and horrifying death, with special emphasis on 'immediate' and 'horrifying.' Whatever else people may say about you, I do know that you are wise enough not to risk a tragedy of such epic proportions. You are simply not the kind of person who would want the brutal murder of anyone, let alone your idolized Clive Endive Ogive IV, on her conscience."

"Yes, I agree," creaked a cautious and meek Esther after only a brief moment. *What else could I say? I* must *find and save President Clive!*

"Excellent. If nothing else, Esther, you have always been a woman of her word. Therefore, please listen carefully. At exactly midnight tonight," Hamish continued, "you will meet me in front of the entrance to the abandoned pump house in the thick woods behind Old Bunbury's fourteenth green. I know that you, unlike most of today's club members and employees, know that this building exists as well as its exact location. You will come alone and will not bring your cell phone or communication device of any other kind. This will be the one and only chance you will have to save the life of a person about whom you care so deeply. Do you understand everything I have just said?"

"Yes," she said, her voice now no more than a nervous whisper. "Is that where I will find President Clive?"

"You will learn the answer to that vexing question quite soon after you arrive," Hamish answered evasively, knowing that he was further incentivizing Esther to act in full accord with his instructions. "Now," Hamish continued with a finality that let Esther know that the conversation, one-sided as it had been, was about to come to its abrupt conclusion, "it is now time for me to steal away and make my final preparations for our midnight rendezvous—a meeting, I must admit, that I have been eagerly anticipating for quite some time." After giving what Esther would have characterized as a diabolical chuckle, Hamish immediately ended the call.

Dazed and befuddled, Esther began to nervously pace the room, unsure as what next to do. Should she ignore what Hamish P. Tumorington had just told her and speak with Detective Giztips? Surely he would know far better than she how to best handle such a dire life-and-death situation. Law enforcement was his chosen profession—a vocation that he dearly loved and at which he so obviously excelled. Or should she heed the threatening and ominous words of Mr. Tumorington, as she had reluctantly agreed, and not tell anyone? Could she risk having President Clive's gruesome and immediate death on her conscience if Hamish somehow discovered that she had failed to comply with his specific demands? Esther realized she was trapped in the classic Catch-22 situation, a horrible quandary in which whatever choice she made might very well lead to unwanted, and perhaps disastrous, consequences.

Esther also realized that if and when she told Detective Giztips about Hamish's call, there could and would be no turning back. It would initiate an irreversible course of action that, for better or worse, would quickly take on a life (or death) of its own. No, Esther concluded, her fierce but short internal debate now finished, she would not yet risk seeing Clive die the "immediate and horrifying death" that Hamish had just so diabolically vowed. Instead, she would forcibly calm herself and try one more time to use her Old Bunbury knowledge, intuitive skills, and deductive powers to find a solution to the considerable dilemma she now faced. It was still more than seven hours until the stroke of midnight, and the ever-optimistic Esther believed that she still had sufficient time to ascertain and carry out an appropriate course of action. *Think, Esther!*

Accordingly, Esther carefully went over, word for word, everything Hamish had told her. Something, her hyperactive brain told her, was amiss, but exactly what it was danced maddingly beyond the grasp of her conscious mind. Like many intuitively smart people, Esther knew that sometimes the best way to recall something specific was to consciously stop trying to recall it. *Just let my subconscious do its usual good work, and the answer will surely swim to the surface.* But would it do so in time?

Esther purposely increased the pace of her walk to a near trot, knowing the physical activity would increase the flow of oxygen to her brain and perhaps, she hoped, jolt her subconscious into providing the desperately sought solution. Her inability to resolve the dilemma she now faced teased her, tantalized her, frustrated her. Esther knew that something Hamish had just said was familiar, a word or turn of phrase that seemed somehow odd and, well, forced. But what was it?

Perhaps, Esther ruminated, Hamish had said something similar when he had surprised her on the streets of Queenstown. *Take your time. Don't force it. Let each and every word that Mr. Tumorington said to you in New Zealand slowly replay in your mind. Pay careful attention to the exact cadence of Hamish's specific words and phrases.*

Wait! she thought excitedly. *Could it be something as simple and seemingly innocuous as* that*?* Could Hamish have been amusing himself all along, taunting her with what he deemed a sort of subtle clue just to make the fiendish game of revenge he apparently deemed himself playing, at least from his warped perspective, somehow more challenging and interesting? Had Mr. Tumorington completely lost his battle with runaway hubris—or worse, total madness?

A wildly excited, frantically hopeful Esther dashed to her Windows 8-equipped HP Pavilion desktop computer and began to type various words into the Google search engine that graced her home page. Twelve minutes of straightforward research and three telephone calls later, Esther was confident that she was on the right track towards solving what surely would be the biggest and most important challenge of her storied life. She realized, of course, that, depending on what she discovered, difficult choices and accompanying differing courses of action still lay ahead; however, Esther also knew that acting on her own on was, at this point, her best chance of rescuing President Clive and seeing that Mr. Tumorington was promptly recaptured and returned to jail. The more she thought about it, the more Esther also became convinced that she had determined the correct course of action for saving her own life as well.

Esther has always been one of those rare people able to think in this manner.

Chapter 28

Showdown

At precisely eight minutes to midnight, Esther pulled into the specially designated, and now totally deserted, employee section of the Old Bunbury Golf Links & Reading Club's reasonably well-lit parking lot. Nerves jangling, heart palpitating, and skin perspiring, Esther was nonetheless confident that she had properly prepared to the very best of her ability for what she fervently hoped would be her final confrontation with Hamish P. Tumorington. Taking purposeful, from-the-diaphragm breaths in an attempt to calm herself, Esther turned off the powerful engine of the unfamiliar silver 2013 CTS-V Cadillac sedan, unlocked and opened the driver's-side front door, and stepped out into the bone-chilling night. The thick, low-lying nimbus clouds, seeping their steady, windswept rain, sent an uncontrollable atavistic shiver down the length of her spine. In a futile attempt to fend off the oppressive dampness and penetrating cold, Esther pulled up the zipper of the dark-blue moisture-proof down parka to within half an inch of her neck. *Let's get on with this.*

Slowly, methodically, Esther tromped through the thick undergrowth in the dense virgin forest behind the fourteenth green toward the abandoned Old Bunbury golf course irrigation pump house. She knew exactly where she was going, although it had been decades since she had last visited this isolated place. The remnants of the once regularly traveled combination gravel and compacted dirt golf cart path were already well on their way towards losing their inevitable clash with the natural process of revegetation. Esther purposely did nothing to disguise the loud rustling and heavy crunching of her steady approach, intent upon Hamish hearing her long before she reached her destination.

When she was thirty feet from the small, paint-peeled front door of the dilapidated, long-abandoned building, Esther stopped and called out softly, "Mr. Tumorington, I have arrived. I have come alone, as promised, in accordance with your specific instructions."

Without warning, the old pump-house door creaked open, and out stepped a menacingly smiling, armed Hamish P. Tumorington. Pointing his Smith & Wesson Bodyguard .38-caliber revolver directly at her smallish chest, he said, "I am happy to see that you have arrived right on time, Esther. Candidly, adhering to schedules of any sort has never been your strong point. I assume that you have followed my instructions to the letter, notifying no one about this meeting and coming alone with neither your cell phone nor communication device of any other kind."

"Yes, sir, indeed I have," Esther answered cautiously, doing her best to steady herself and project an air of confidence that she did not really feel.

"Excellent. I was quite confident that you would fully comply."

"Where is Mr. Ogive? You promised if I acted in accordance with your specific demands that you would tell me where he is."

"Indeed I did, Esther. Indeed I did," he said. "You were also always someone, as I recall, who did not like to beat around the proverbial bush—a characteristic that, I must admit, I have always greatly admired in people. Far too many, especially in the world of private clubs, are unwilling and afraid to speak the pure and unadulterated truth; instead, they are focused on, and guided by, silly, obsolete rules, getting along, and being politically correct. In answer to your pressing question, your beloved President Clive is currently inside the abandoned pump house you now face, gagged and tied in a manner that prevents him from either crying out or escaping."

"And why should I believe you, Mr. Tumorington?"

"A fair question, Esther. Just follow me inside the building, and you will promptly see that I am telling the unadulterated truth."

"I don't think so, Mr. Tumorington. Once I am inside the confines of that decrepit, claustrophobic structure, nothing good can happen. Accordingly, I have an alternate suggestion. Please go back inside and remove President Clive's gag so that he may call out to me, proving that what you have just said is genuine and that you have caused Old Bunbury's revered leader no bodily injury. Once I hear that he is alive and unharmed, I give you my word that I will accompany you, should you so desire, inside the pump house."

"Ah, ever the skeptical Esther. But you do make a valid point, at least from your perspective, and I see no harm in agreeing to your request. No one other than the three of us is currently on the Old Bunbury grounds, and even if Clive screams maniacally for help, no one other than the two of us will hear. Besides, I am totally confident that having this gun pointing at his head, in combination with my threat to shoot you immediately should he actually scream, will prevent him from making unnecessarily loud and unwanted cries for help. Please remain exactly where you are, Esther; in short order, you will hear the voice of your beloved Clive Endive Ogive IV."

"I am not going anywhere, Mr. Tumorington," said Esther. "Of that you can be certain."

Less than a minute later, Esther heard the muffled but sufficiently distinguishable voice that she so longed to hear. "Esther! Are you out there? Why on earth did you come to this godforsaken place?"

"I am here to save you," came the increasingly confident voice of Old Bunbury's most famous waitress. Hamish P. Tumorington, who had just reemerged from the building, gave Esther a quizzical look as the surprisingly self-assured tone of her voice registered with his racing, demented brain.

"Are you alright, boss?" Esther shouted, her confidence continuing to grow.

"I'm okay, Esther, but you have to run. Now!" President Clive implored. "Hamish, lying scum that he is, has lured you here under false pretenses. He drugged and kidnapped me and brought me here only to tempt you into eventually following. Hamish's intentions all along have been to kill the both of us for our part in his arrest and conviction for Alfie Johnson's murder. He told me so himself." The primitive, infectious panic in his voice was palpable.

"To the contrary, Esther. I suggest you stay exactly where you are," spat Hamish P. Tumorington, his revolver now pointed directly at her chest. "But alas, I must admit that your doomed hero is indeed correct in all he has just told you. My plan has always been to gather the both of you together at this hidden-away spot on the hallowed grounds of your beloved Old Bunbury and mercilessly gun you down like rabid dogs gone amok. What better delicious irony could there ever be—*ever*—than to watch the two people most responsible for sending me to prison die on the property of their very favorite private club in the entire world! Just so you know, Esther, I am going to end your miserably meddlesome life first so Clive can experience the acute pain and bitter anguish of your abrupt demise. His turn to meet his maker will come soon enough after you have gone to the great private club in the sky—assuming, of course, that the celestial admission committee acts favorably upon your weak application. And now, my dear Esther, without further discussion, I must bid you adieu."

The flashes of Hamish's gun lit up the dreary night, and its accompanying blasts echoed off the surrounding majestic oaks, elms, and maples. Hamish had aimed directly at the center of Esther's torso and, with great satisfaction, twice pulled the trigger of his Smith & Wesson revolver. To his pure shock and utter astonishment, however, Esther remained standing, an angelic smile beginning to spread across her determined, increasingly confident face. "What?"

Hamish wailed. "I know that this gun was pointed directly at your wizened, blinded-by-loyalty heart. I am absolutely positive that both bullets should have been direct and fatal hits. How can it be that you are still standing?"

"Alas, Mr. Tumorington, I regret to inform you that the handgun you have just fired is loaded with blanks. Accordingly, I suggest that you put down your weapon, lie down flat on the ground, and surrender immediately to me." With that, Esther reached into the right pocket of her parka, pulled out her semiautomatic Smith & Wesson Model 39, and took dead aim. "Let me assure you that the ammunition in this particular gun, unlike yours, is as real as it can be."

"Esther. Y*ou* have a gun? Since when did you get a gun? What do you even *know* about guns?"

"For starters, Mr. Tumorington, I know that, while your toadies have done extensive research on me, they have not been as thorough as you might have hoped. Very few people, if any, now alive know that my dearly departed father taught me how to shoot—and shoot well—when I was just a little girl. Although I now rarely carry a weapon on my person—I suspect that your henchmen also failed to discover that I have quietly maintained my concealed weapons permit since I first acquired it over a half century ago—I am quite confident that I remain a decent enough marksman to send you to an early grave if you do not immediately drop your useless firearm and lie flat on the ground. I *will* shoot you, Mr. Tumorington, if you try anything, anything at all."

"Noooooooooo," Hamish wailed, his primeval ululations echoing through the cold, dark night. "How could this have happened? My plans for sweet revenge were perfect, absolutely perfect." With feral, irrational rage, Hamish P. Tumorington pointed his gun directly at Esther's chest and squeezed off four more rounds, all with the same ineffectual result. Esther remained standing where she was, her handgun unwaveringly centered on Hamish's chest. "Please, Mr.

Tumorington, I do not wish to harm you, but I repeat for the last time: I will shoot if you do not immediately drop your weapon and lie on the ground. *Now*."

If any vestige of rationality or human decency had remained within Hamish up until this point in time, the last of it had now clearly dissipated; the man, his maniacally flailing arms, soullessly glaring eyes, demonically inhuman grin, and screechily primeval voice confirmed, had gone totally berserk. Glaring menacingly at Esther, he shrilled, "I am going to kill you and Clive, if I have too, with the butt of this pistol. Neither of you deserves to live for what you have done to me. If necessary, I will happily bludgeon you both to death with my bare hands or with one of the rusted steel bars left behind in the old pump house you are now facing. Enough of this! Die, Esther, die!" With that, Hamish began a mad, savage dash directly towards her, his sole focus on fulfilling his demented promise.

When Hamish P. Tumorington was fifteen feet away and closing fast, she knew she had no other choice. Esther took dead aim and fired.

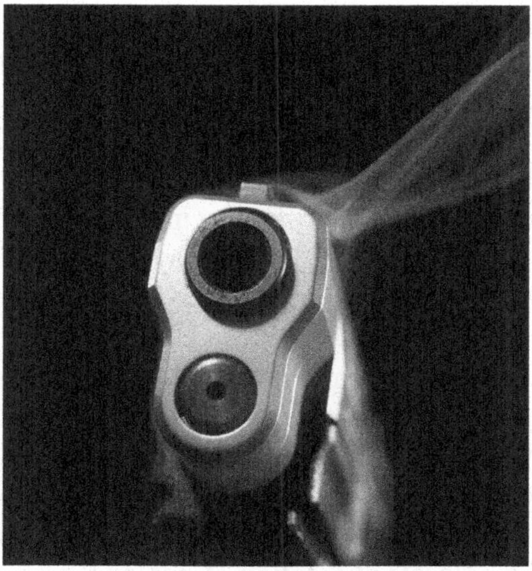

A girl's gotta do what a girl's gotta do.

Chapter 29

A Flurry of Activity

The forward momentum of Hamish P. Tumorington's frenzied charge carried him to within a yard of Esther's solidly planted feet, where he finally dropped to the ground, writhing in sheer agony. His right kneecap was a thing of the past.

"I thought you said you could shoot!" Hamish wailed, looking up dazedly at Esther as both his hands, covered in a gory mixture of blood, bone, tendon, and cartilage, clutched what little remained of the middle part of his right leg. "You missed so badly when you fired that you hit me in the knee!" he screeched in an almost inhuman, high-pitched frenzy.

"To the contrary, Mr. Tumorington," said Esther said stolidly. "I hit you precisely where I was aiming. My intent was to prevent you from killing me, not send you to an early grave."

Staring up at Esther's still smoking gun from his contorted, near-fetal position, Hamish pleaded, between his continuing tortured moans, "If you are really that good of a marksman, Esther, then I beg of you, please finish the job. Tap me once between the eyes and twice in the heart just to be sure. I simple cannot go back to jail. If nothing else, do it for the love of the golfing gods and as a favor to this former Old Bunbury member, the private club that you cherish most in the entire world."

"Mr. Tumorington, I must say that your request is quite tempting, considering all that you have put President Clive, Old Bunbury, and me through. However, even though we live in an Obama-sanctioned and government-enabled environment of increasing moral depravity, ungrounded ethical relativism, transgenerational cultural disintegration, Orwellian overregulation and bureaucracy, skyrocketing historical illiteracy, wanton discard of time-tested cultural mores, and wholesale abdication of personal responsibility, I myself cannot and will not descend into such a primitive level of existence. As civilized people, both you and I know that murder, in and of itself, is absolutely and unconditionally *wrong*. It always has been and always will be. Period. End of story. I shot you in the right kneecap precisely because I am a good enough shot to hit you exactly where I was aiming; I purposely positioned my bullet to disable but not kill. You are going back to jail for the remainder of your wretched life."

"For what it's worth, I do know in my heart of hearts that, at least on this particular subject so fundamentally crucial to the very survival of the best parts of human civilization, you are absolutely and inarguably correct," whispered Hamish, already deep into his slide towards a state of incomprehensible wailing and inchoate semiconsciousness.

Has my strategically placed bullet somehow jolted Hamish back to the world of sanity and rationality? Esther wondered. *Has the man now rediscovered his core humanity?* Perhaps, despite the Obamas of the world, there was real hope for mankind after all.

As if on cue, Esther heard the distant but most welcome voice of Detective Adam Giztips calling frantically from what she guessed to be the Old Bunbury employee parking lot. "Esther! Where are you? Are you *alright*? We heard *shots*!"

"I'm fine, Detective," Esther shouted back. "More importantly, so is President Clive! He is unharmed but tied up in the golf course irrigation pump house. Mr. Tumorington, however, has not fared as well. Please call an ambulance for him immediately. I had no choice but to wound him in the kneecap. The good news is that, with proper medical attention, he will live to face a long and miserable life in a federal maximum-security facility."

By the time Esther had finished speaking, Detective Giztips and his two accompanying officers had successfully followed the sound of her voice and made their way to the fateful scene.

"Esther! Thank goodness you are safe!" Detective Giztips gasped, giving her a gentle hug, the kind of platonic embrace often shared by people who, over time, have become close. One of the accompanying officers, Sergeant Karen Wilken, was already attending to the now unconscious Hamish P. Tumorington while the other, Patrolman Patrick Bonfield, had already dashed into the pump house to find and free Clive.

"Why didn't you call me for help, Esther? You could have been hurt or killed!" said Detective Giztips, the stern, unwavering tone of his chastising voice not lost on her.

"I did what I thought best, Detective, to both find and save the life of President Clive. "If there were any other possible way, any way at all, I surely would have spoken directly with you. I know you know that to be true."

Just then, Officer Bonfield emerged from the small pump house holding a wobbly, dirt-covered, haggard-looking Clive Endive Ogive IV.

"Esther saved me, Adam. She save the both of us. She is a real hero," Clive said as he, with tears falling, gave one of his all-time favorite people in the entire world a long, grateful caress. Thank you, young lady. Thank you so very much."

"No worries, boss," said Esther with a big toothy smile. "You would have done the same thing for me."

"I agree with your sentiments, Clive," added Detective Giztips. "No matter how foolish and rash our dear Esther can be at times, she is nonetheless someone whose unbridled courage and incontestable nobility are beyond question."

Changing the subject, Detective Giztips asked, "So how are *you* doing, my friend? I've seen people on skid row who have looked better—but having said that, you are indeed a sight for sore eyes."

"Thanks," answered Clive, an incongruous grin breaking out upon his utterly exhausted face. "I'm still a bit woozy from the drugs Hamish kept injecting. My pride, I must admit, is also a bit wounded, and I cannot recall when I was last such a sartorial disaster, but, other than that, I feel quite well, considering the circumstances. I should be back on the golf course in a day or two. I've been on quite a hot streak, you know."

"We'll see about that," said the ever-cautious detective. "I am going to have one of my officers escort you to the hospital for observation. I want to hear the doctors, not you, confirm that you are as healthy as you claim to be. And I don't want to hear one word of protest from you. Not a peep."

"Speaking of hospitals, Detective Giztips, we need to get this one there as soon as possible," said Officer Wilken, nodding at the ashen face of Hamish P. Tumorington. "He has already lost a lot of blood."

"The ambulance should be here any minute," said Detective Giztips. "There, listen. I can hear the sirens in the distance. Officer Bonfield, I suggest you head back to the parking lot to meet the paramedics and quickly lead them here," he continued. "Officer Wilken will continue to attend to Mr. Tumorington, and I will begin calling for appropriate backup."

The next thirty minutes were a comfortable blur to Esther, who sat quietly to the side as the police and paramedics went about their good work. Three additional officers and five crime scene investigative specialists also joined the group over the course of that half hour and began their meticulous, well-practiced, and efficiently coordinated efforts at securing and examining the crime scene. It was clear that their initial investigation would not be over any time soon. Hamish had already been rushed to the hospital, accompanied by Officer Wilken—the police were taking absolutely no chances on another escape—and Clive driven there separately in the patrol car of one of the assisting officers. Esther watched Detective Giztips supervise the entire operation with a professional pride, depth of expertise, and wealth of experience that made her proud.

When he was fully confident that everything was proceeding as it should, Detective Giztips walked over to where

Esther was sitting and said, "Esther, I am now going to take you home so you can get a good night's rest. It's clear that you have had an extremely difficult and challenging day. Please meet me at my office tomorrow morning promptly at eight so I can take your statement. In the meantime, I advise you not to speak with anyone—except, if you so choose, with your lawyer—about what happened here this evening. I will need to know everything—and I do mean *everything*—you did from the time you successfully ditched the policemen who was assigned to watch over you until the time I arrived here earlier this evening."

"Fair enough, Detective," said Esther. "I will be there precisely at eight. I do hope that the good officer assigned to protect me won't get into any trouble. I only did what I had to do to save President Clive's life."

"We shall see, Esther. Let's go home."

More than a few believe that the secret headquarters of the New Zealand ovine revolutionary leaders is hidden in the humanly inaccessible mountains around Mount Cook.

Chapter 30

Explanations

Esther arrived at the pragmatically yet tastefully furnished office of Detective Adam Giztips a few minutes before eight, fully prepared and eager to report every possible detail she could recall about her frightening denouement with Hamish P. Tumorington. She couldn't be sure, of course, but suspected that what she fervently hoped and believed would be a cathartic unburdening would take up most, if not all, of the morning; Detective Giztips, if nothing else, gave new meaning to thorough.

"Good morning, Esther," Adam Giztips said cordially as, ever the gentleman, he simultaneously pulled back a wheeled tan office chair for her. "I hope you were able to get some rest."

"Surprisingly, Detective, I slept like a baby. It is such a relief to know that Hamish P. Tumorington is back in the good custody of the police. Speaking of Mr. Tumorington, how is the person who emptied his Smith & Wesson Bodyguard .38-caliber revolver at me late last night faring?"

"He'll live, Esther. The doctors did all they could to repair his shattered right kneecap but agree that he will surely need a prosthesis and months, if not years, of arduous rehabilitative work before he comes close to once again walking normally. More importantly, he remains under the constant surveillance of a crack team of federal agents who will ensure that this heinous murderer never again sets foot in public."

"That is very good news, Detective. For what it's worth, while I am certainly personally relieved and happy for all concerned that Mr. Tumorington is once again safely behind bars, I must tell you that I harbor no festering ill will towards the man. Life is just too short."

"You are a better person than most," said Detective Giztips admiringly.

Deftly changing the topic, Esther continued, "I heard that President Clive is doing well. Other than suffering a relatively mild case of dehydration and some assorted minor scratches and bruises, Old Bunbury's esteemed leader appears to be as fit as the proverbial fiddle for a man of his, shall we say, advancing age. I understand that the hospital released him early this morning and he is already back at home resting comfortably."

"It's good to see that your encyclopedic knowledge of all things Old Bunbury remains intact, Esther. It is indeed true what they say: Nothing, absolutely nothing, ever gets past you when it comes to your favorite private club on the planet. It is also wonderful news that what could have been a unmitigated disaster, likely one involving multiple murders, turned out as well as it did. But enough with the preliminaries, Esther. I would appreciate it if you would now take me through, step by step, your part in this tragic tale."

"Certainly, Detective," agreed Esther graciously, "Let us begin on this past Thursday afternoon, starting with the time I left Old Bunbury. After calling everyone I could think of who might know the whereabouts of President Clive, I drove straight home, more worried than ever, that something bad, really bad, had happened to him. It just wasn't like the boss, I knew, to seemingly disappear from the face of the earth with telling at least *someone*. Obviously, my first thought was that Hamish P. Tumorington had secretly made his way back to town and was somehow responsible for Mr. Ogive's unexplained absence—a most reasonable assumption, I am sure you will agree.

"Other than Clive's second and third ex-wives, everyone with whom I had spoken earlier in the day had appeared genuinely concerned about President Clive's sudden and inexplicable disappearance. At first I thought that Caddy Maddie or Clem the Gem might have had something to do with it. Oh, Detective, please, my sincerest apologies," interjected Esther meekly, seemingly embarrassed at what she deemed a social faux pas. "Those are the nicknames that the Old Bunbury members and staff have given Madison MacLaine (nee Brennan) Ogive and Clemencia Tabatha (nee Snerdly) Ogive."

"No worries, Esther," Detective Giztips said with a smile.

Quickly gathering herself, Esther pressed on. "As I was saying, I soon enough relegated these two ladies' overt hostility to nothing more than the understandable bitterness of two money-grubbing hussies who had been unceremoniously dumped when President Clive finally wised up and stopped thinking with the wrong part of his anatomy. He isn't the first male, and certainly won't be the last, to have made that particular mistake," Esther added sardonically. "No, this just *had* to be the work of Hamish P. Tumorington."

"While I was pondering what next to do, my cell rang. I looked and saw, with great excitement, that it was President Clive's personal number. I remember my immediate feeling of relief and delight; I was sure Mr. Ogive was calling to assure me that everything was alright. You can therefore well understand my utter dismay when I heard the villainous voice of Hamish P. Tumorington on the other end of the line."

"Yes, Esther," Detective Giztips interjected. "We have already run Clive's recent telephone records. We knew that *someone* had called your cell from that number this past Thursday afternoon. What we didn't know was that it was the nefarious Hamish P. Tumorington. Please continue."

"Mr. Tumorington told me, in no uncertain terms, that he had kidnapped President Clive and was holding him hostage in the abandoned golf course pump house station at Old Bunbury," she resumed. "He added that my one and only chance of saving President Clive from a brutal and immediate death was to tell absolutely no one—I repeat, *no one*—about his call and to meet him at the pump house at midnight, alone and without communication devices of any kind. I thought long and hard about telephoning you then and there, but, at the end of the day, I knew I simply could not take the risk of failing to comply with Hamish's specific instructions. As you well know, Mr. Tumorington is a *very* wealthy and well-connected man and has been able, through his cadre of highly paid toadies, to garner all sorts of insider information about you, me, and everyone involved in the ongoing attempt to bring him to justice. In the end, I weighed the pros and cons and opted for what I deemed to be the most prudent course of action."

"Given the circumstances, Esther, I certainly understand your reluctance to inform the authorities," said a somber Detective Giztips after a moment had elapsed. "However, in virtually *all* cases, it is better to seek immediate professional help in such matters. I repeat: It is indeed most fortunate that things turned out as well as they did."

"Thank you, Detective. I am certain that you are correct. Let's just hope that such a horrific choice is never again foisted upon me."

"With that I could not agree more," he said. "Please continue."

"As I was saying, I kept replaying in my mind everything Mr. Tumorington had said, both in Queenstown and on President Clive's cell phone. My intuition, a facility which I like to believe is reasonably well honed, told me that *something* was amiss. I found it extremely frustrating that, for a time, I simply could not put my finger on it. And then, out of the blue, it hit me—one of those rare and wonderful aha! moments when everything just seems to fall into place. Mr. Tumorington, I deduced, was taunting me with a sort of subtle clue, probably amusing himself all along and thinking that I was simply not clever enough to solve his little puzzle. In retrospect, of course, it turned out that he was sadly mistaken."

"So, I will gladly take the bait, Esther. What exactly did Hamish say that caused, shall we say, your sleuthing enlightenment?" asked an obviously excited Detective Giztips.

"The very last thing Mr. Tumorington told me in Queenstown was that it was time for him to, quote, *steal* away—an odd turn of phrase, to be sure. The final words out of his mouth during this past Thursday's telephone conversation were *exactly* the same: It was time for him to *steal* away. It was just too much of a coincidence for these two exact, strangely worded phrases to occur in both conversations. I knew immediately that the word 'steal' had to be the key.

"As I recall, I had to take a series of deep breaths to calm myself," Esther continued. "Thinking things through, I knew that, since Mr. Tumorington planned on meeting me at Old Bunbury at twelve o'clock, he had to be relatively close; our scheduled pump-house midnight rendezvous was only hours away. Where was the most likely place for him to be staying? I asked myself. Probably not at his own house, the home of a trusted friend, a close family member, or even a hotel or motel near a major highway, I concluded. All far too risky. With that, I turned on my computer and did a Google search for the names of all the off-the-beaten-path motels, hotels, and bed-and-breakfast establishments within twenty-five miles of Old Bunbury, pairing my search with the word steal—and assorted spelling variations thereof. Eureka! It turned out there was only one: Steele's Family Motel & RV Park."

"I know the place, Esther," Detective Giztips interrupted. "It's not more than ten or twelve miles from Old Bunbury in what is now a seedy, unsafe, and judiciously avoided part of town. In many ways, it would be the ideal place for Hamish to hole up."

"I had exactly the same thought," said Esther excitedly. "After that, it became more and more apparent what I had to do. First, I realized that, if I were to successfully carry out the plan that was rapidly taking shape in my mind, I needed to escape the watchful eye of the well-intentioned officer you had assigned to protect me. He would surely have informed you immediately about any seemingly suspicious movements on my part. Accordingly, I called my next-door neighbor and longtime great friend, Cheryl Anderson, to ask if I could borrow her car, no questions asked. I was confident that Cheryl would help—and she did. She dropped off her new Cadillac 2013 CTS-V Cadillac sedan—a fantastic ride, by the way—near the south entrance to the Tri-County Mall, leaving the door unlocked and keys under the mat. I reminded her that she could, if she so chose, remain nearby to keep tabs on her vehicle until she saw me get in and drive away. After that, it was a simple matter for Cheryl to flag down one of the many taxis at either mall entrance and take the relatively short ride home."

"So *that's* how you got away," said Detective Giztips admiringly. "The last time Officer Charles Hambrook saw you was when you parked your car near the mall's north entrance and sauntered in. He made the quite reasonable assumption that you were making some sort of routine purchase and would return to your vehicle shortly. Charlie had no reason to suspect, none whatsoever, that you in the process of ditching him."

"That is correct," said Esther. "So you can now see why I believe that Officer Hambrook should not get into any trouble for his actions."

"Agreed," said Detective Giztips. "Just so you know," he added, "we ran the Cadillac's license plate last night after you had gone home. When we called the owner, Ms. Anderson was most cooperative and told us exactly what you have just said. Her biggest concern, by the way, was for your safety. She was *very* relieved to hear that you were okay. You are lucky to have such a wonderful friend, Esther. Not long after that, an officer drove Ms. Anderson's car from the Old Bunbury employee parking lot back to her home. Using the spare key given to us by Ms. Anderson, we also made sure that your car was picked up at the mall and safely returned."

"So *that's* how my car found its way back to my driveway!" said Esther gratefully. "Thank you very much, Detective Giztips. I suspected something along those lines. But once again, back to the story.

"My next step," Esther resumed resolutely, "was to call an old buddy from high school, Arnie Archeson, the longtime owner of Arnie's Ammo & Assault Accessories over on Fourth Avenue. I asked him to do me a special last-minute favor, and he readily agreed."

"And this, I assume, was to place your order for faux bullets," Detective Giztips said quite matter-of-factly. As a temporarily befuddled Esther sat and stared, he quickly pressed on. "The shell casings and charred remnants of crimped wadding—material typically used to hold the gunpowder against the primer in blank bullets—we found at the scene of the crime, in combination with the fact that no real bullet slugs have as yet been discovered in the nearby trees, strongly suggest that Hamish's gun was loaded with blanks. Ballistics will tell us more in a few days."

"That is excellent police work, Detective," beamed Esther. "Congratulations!"

"We are not exactly amateurs, Esther," Detective Giztips said drolly.

"I certainly meant no offense," Esther quickly apologized, her face turning a bright crimson.

"None taken, Esther. Please relax, young lady. You know that I was just teasing you. I can't wait to hear how it came to be that blanks found their way into Hamish's gun." Smiling, Detective Giztips said, "Please continue."

"I drove Cheryl's car," said Esther, once again composing herself and picking up where she had left off, "after having first gathered several items from home on the off chance that they might later prove helpful, to pick up the blanks that Arnie had prepared for me. He had made enough dummy cartridges to fill virtually any kind of .22-, .38-, or

.45-caliber gun. I was, of course, guessing that if Hamish had a firearm, it would more than likely hold one of these three most common bullet sizes. From there, I drove directly to Steele's Family Motel & RV Park. When I arrived, I remained in the car and made another call, this time to the motel office, where I asked to speak with Mr. Steal in room nine. Thankfully, the gruff, indifferent voice on the other end of the line—the owner or night manager, I presumed—didn't ask me how to spell the name. Instead, he nonchalantly corrected me—just what I was hoping for—telling me that Mr. Steal was in room ten and, without further delay, put me through to the room. Before the first ring started, I had already hung up."

"Why did you do that, Esther?" Detective Giztips asked.

"Well, I didn't want Mr. Tumorington, if he was indeed in the room, to hear his telephone ring. Presumably, no one had a clue as to where he was hiding, and the last thing I wanted to do was spook him. Instead, I got out of the car and slowly, cautiously edged my way closer to room ten. When I was less than six feet away, I could see that all the lights were off."

"And then what did you do?"

"I must admit that I, for the moment, I was stumped. It once again crossed my mind that perhaps it was now time to get in touch with you. It was likely that I had pinpointed Mr. Tumorington's hideout and that you and your fellow policemen could and would surely recapture him in short order. However, since no one yet knew *for sure* President Clive's whereabouts and whether he was *really* alive and unharmed—Mr. Tumorington, I knew, could very well have been lying about everything he had told me—I once again decided against that particular course of action.

"After returning to Cheryl's car to ponder my next steps, I happened to notice that, other than me, there was only one other car in the entire parking lot, and it was parked directly in front of the motel office. It surely had to be the owner or night manager's personal vehicle. Considering both the lack of lights in room ten and the absence of any nearby car, I made a bold decision: I would sneak into Hamish P. Tumorington's room. Accordingly, I got of the car, walked to the door of room ten, and, penknife, small screwdriver, and safety pin in hand and flashlight in my pocket—all items that I had purposely brought from home—began to jimmy the lock. I had the cheaply made old-fashioned lock picked, I am proud to say, in less than thirty seconds."

"That was a very risky move on your part," said Detective Giztips.

"Yes, I know it was, but I was desperate," said Esther. "Just to be safe, I did bring one of my handguns along with me, Detective. I may at times be a bit rash, but I don't consider myself foolish."

"For the moment, I'll defer commenting on *that*," said Detective Giztips wryly. "If you don't mind, Esther, I think that this would be the perfect time for a ten-minute break."

"I agree," said Esther. "I don't know about you, but my three cups of morning java seem to have caught up with me. We both know that, in the end, people do not own their daily caffeine fixes; they only rent them."

Unlike Hamish P. Tumorington, most patrons of the Steele Family Motel & RV Park opt for the hourly rate.

Chapter 31

Explanations—Continued

When both Esther and Adam had returned to the good detective's office and taken their respective seats, Esther promptly carried on with her tale.

"Back to my story, Detective," she began without preliminaries. "I still have quite a bit to tell. Once I heard the motel room's flimsy door lock click open, I quickly put away my faux locksmith tools and replaced them with a loaded Smith & Wesson Model 39 in my right hand and a flashlight in my left. It was now or never, I clearly remember thinking to myself. Gathering my courage, I switched on the flashlight, pushed opened the paint-chipped feeble door, and confidently stepped into what I believed to be an empty room."

"Esther, did it occur to you that Hamish might have been hiding, perhaps in the bathroom or the clothes closet?" asked Detective Giztips, the concern for her well-being obvious.

"As a matter of fact, Detective, it did. That was exactly why I held my cocked pistol waist high, aimed straight ahead; if necessary, I was fully prepared to shoot. I quickly scanned the dilapidated excuse for a motel room with my flashlight and saw that the tiny, cramped quarters had no closet of any kind, only a couple of cheap open-wire shelves precariously perched atop a thin beige plastic clothes rod strewn with twisted, mismatched wire hangers. At the far end of the room stood an old-fashioned free-standing sink—the kind with separate spigots for the hot and cold water. The small door to the immediate left of the sink, presumably the entrance to the toilet, was wide open. I cautiously moved forward, pistol pointed always where it should, until I could see that the cramped toilet space was also empty. No, it was clear that the room, except for me, was unoccupied."

"What did you do next?" asked Detective Giztips, his fascination with her sleuthing powers continuing to grow.

"Well, I had to move quickly, since I knew that Mr. Tumorington might very well return at any moment. Glancing around the room, I saw what I presumed to be his revolver atop the small wooden nightstand and, next to that, a passport."

"His passport?" interrupted Detective Giztips. "No passport was found either on Mr. Tumorington or at the scene of the crime. In fact, we found no identification of any sort."

"Please, Detective Giztips, I will get to that in a moment," said Esther, slightly annoyed at the interruption. "Working as fast as these incipiently arthritic hands would allow, I replaced the real .38-caliber bullets in Mr. Tumorington's gun with the appropriate blanks that my friend Arnie had crafted for me earlier that same evening. From all his years of membership at Old Bunbury, I knew full well that Mr. Tumorington understood virtually nothing about firearms. Accordingly, I was reasonably certain that, even if he double-checked the pistol later on to make sure it was loaded, he would not recognize the difference between real bullets and the dummies. I was confident, although I obviously did not yet know the specifics, that Mr. Tumorington's now-useless gun would give me a huge advantage when the two of us met later that evening.

"Then and only then, Detective, did I open the passport. I saw that Mr. Tumorington was apparently traveling under the alias of one Rich V. Steele. The name immediately struck me as odd, but at the time, I didn't give it any further thought; my task at hand, I knew, was to leave the room exactly as I had found it and skedaddle. On my way out the door, I did notice that Mr. Tumorington's luggage was fully packed and sitting atop the unmade, junk-food-wrapper–covered bed, ready to be transported at a moment's notice. Whatever happened later that night, it was clear that Mr. Tumorington wasn't planning to remain in this room."

"I see, Esther," said Detective Giztips. "And then what did you do?"

"Since it was still more than two hours before our midnight rendezvous at Old Bunbury's abandoned pump house, I drove over to the Lincoln State Preserve & Recreational Area and parked in the far lot near the boat-launching facilities. I knew I had to go somewhere where no one would think to look for me. As I sat there, I carefully went over in my mind what I calculated to be the best way to deal with Mr. Tumorington when he and I met. After a time, I was confident that I had prepared, to the very best of my ability, for all contingencies. I also thought a lot about the assumed name under which Mr. Tumorington had apparently been traveling: Rich V. Steele. 'Steele,' I deduced, seemed to make sense, as it matched the name of the motel in which Mr. Tumorington had chosen to stay. It was clearly more than coincidence; the word, if nothing else, told me that Mr. Tumorington had carefully researched and meticulously planned each and every move since his escape from prison. He knew well in advance that Steele's Family Motel & RV Park existed and that it would be the perfect place to hole up when he returned from New Zealand to the Old Bunbury environs. But just who, exactly, was Rich? What was the significance of *that* particular name? Why only Rich and not Richard? And why did Hamish opt for only a middle initial and not a full middle name? What was the importance of the capital letter V? Why not another letter?

"For a long time, my racing mind simply could not make a lick of sense of the latest conundrum that Mr. Tumorington had inadvertently left for me. Perhaps, I told myself, I was overthinking the entire situation; maybe the name was nothing more than a randomly chosen alias. No, I quickly reminded myself, I knew Mr. Tumorington far too well from his many years as an Old Bunbury member to know that this simply would not be the case. It had to be some sort of clever puzzle or play on words, something that he personally found amusing. And then, like my sudden revelation earlier in the day, it hit me like the proverbial ton of bricks!"

"Esther, I will gladly yield to your considerable powers of deduction," said Detective Giztips. "What *is* the special significance of the name Rich V. Steele?"

"It is really quite simple, Detective. Then again, all good puzzles are simple once one knows the solution. The letters in the name Rich V. Steele, taken together, are an anagram of the two names Clive and Esther. Nothing more and nothing less. I now knew beyond any shadow of a doubt that the motel room I had just visited was indeed Mr. Tumorington's!"

"Your amazing powers of deduction remain unsurpassed," said a warmly approving Detective Giztips. "Congratulations, Esther! However, it does seem a bit odd to me that our escaped murderer is apparently so obsessed with wordplay."

"It is a trait, Detective Giztips, that he naturally garnered from his many years at Old Bunbury," Esther answered. "Bad puns—the kind that make you grimace and groan—assorted wordplay and clever linguistic puzzles are as much a part of Old Bunbury's unique history and traditions as are its bizarrely stringent requirements for membership and punishingly severe restrictions on guest usage of any kind. It's just another one of the many idiosyncrasies that make Old Bunbury so wonderfully special. Apparently, Mr. Tumorington, although no longer a member, just couldn't get that particular aspect of the club's wonderfully enchanting culture out of his system."

"I see," said Detective Giztips, fascinated by all he was continuing to learn about the zany world of private clubs.

"After that, I basically rested in my car until it was time to make the drive to Old Bunbury for what I fervently hoped would be my final meeting with Mr. Tumorington,"

Esther continued. With her characteristically unremitting attention to detail and considerable linguistic prowess, Esther carefully related everything that had happened from the time she had pulled in to the employee section of the Old Bunbury parking lot until Detective Giztips and his two fellow policemen had arrived on the scene of the crime. Detective Giztips was so completely engaged in her captivating tale that he did not interrupt a single time.

When Esther had finally finished, Detective Giztips said admiringly, "That is quite a story, Esther. You surely could have been killed, young lady. What if Hamish had reloaded his pistol with live ammunition?"

"Obviously, that most worrisome thought crossed my mind more than once," she said wistfully, "but I knew that Hamish, even in the *very* unlikely event that he had so acted, still couldn't hit the broad side of a barn from thirty feet. This was a man, as I previously explained, who knew virtually nothing about guns. Candidly, I would be surprised if, up to the time of our fateful encounter, he had ever discharged a firearm of any kind over the course of his über-privileged and highly sheltered life. Plus, once he fired his first two bullets, I knew with absolute certainty that Mr. Tumorington was—please excuse the double entendre—shooting blanks. Those of us who have sufficient expertise in and experience with firearms can easily recognize that distinctive whooshing sound of a real bullet as it exits the barrel of a gun. In addition, I heard no dull whomps of any kind, the sort of sound that that one would normally expect from a live round colliding with one of the many trees behind me. No, I was more confident than ever that Mr. Tumorington's remaining bullets were nothing more than useless blanks."

"Fair enough, Esther," said Detective Giztips. "I must say, you certainly know your firearms," he added admiringly.

"Despite the unending distortions and despicable lies we are spoon-fed daily by the far too many rabid Second

Amendment haters populating this still-great country, I firmly believe that it is the inalienable right and core responsibility of every single American to learn all they can about guns," said Esther proudly. "Only by so doing can we guarantee our continuing freedom and liberty in the years and decades to come."

"Amen to that," agreed Detective Giztips with a fervor that made Esther proud to call him a loyal and trusted friend.

"If I may," Detective Giztips continued, "I would like to ask a few more questions before you take your leave. You have been exceedingly cooperative and forthright, Esther—and candidly, I expected nothing less. Thank you so very much. Now, as to my additional queries: First, you spoke earlier about Hamish's passport and packed luggage. Presumably, both are in his car. The trouble is, as of this moment, we still have no idea as to the specific make or model or where it might be located."

"I think I can help you with that," said Esther. "Driving past Old Bunbury's entrance earlier today on my way to this meeting, I noticed a strange car parked in Montgomery and Ernesta Quaddlelooper's driveway. It is close to their house and almost totally blocked from view by the exquisitely maintained property's many mature trees and protective hedge lines. So you know, the Quaddleloopers are the long-time Old Bunbury members who own the estate directly across from the club's front entrance. The Quaddleloopers, I know, are currently enjoying the owner's suite aboard Oceania cruise line's fabulous ship *Nautica*. The car on their property, something that I did not notice last evening because of the darkness, certainly does not belong to them. If I had to hazard a guess, I would say that the vehicle might very well be the one Mr. Tumorington has been driving, given its secluded location so near to the club on a property that he most certainly would have known to be temporarily vacant.

At the very least, it is worth further investigation on your part."

"Thank you, Esther. We will get right on it. I have another question for you: If you purposely chose not to tell anyone about all you were up to in the hours immediately preceding your midnight denouement with Hamish, why, then, did you suddenly change your mind and send me a lengthy, precisely worded, grammatically and syntactically perfect text at exactly seven minutes until midnight? Wasn't that cutting it too close for comfort? And what if we had showed up prematurely—*before* you had confronted Hamish and were certain that Clive was alive and unharmed? Would that not have muddled your carefully made plans?"

"A fair question, Detective," Esther said. "Again, the answer is quite simple. I prepared the text well in advance, when I was sitting in my car at the Lincoln State Park & Recreational Area. As you know, I gave you specific details about where I—and I fervently hoped President Clive—could be found. If something had gone wrong with my plan, I certainly didn't want to be responsible for abetting Mr. Tumorington's escape. Accordingly, knowing that it would take you about twelve minutes, at breakneck speed, to make it from either your home or your office to Old Bunbury, I calculated that the proper time for you to receive this text was precisely seven minutes before midnight. In case you are interested, I used an app on my iPhone 5 called TextLater; it allows you to prepare your messages in advance and preset the specific time when they will be sent. Not a bad investment for ninety-nine cents, Detective. I suggest that you look into it."

"Aha! I see. Indeed I will," the good detective chuckled.

"There is one final detail, Detective," said Esther, "that I inadvertently forgot to mention. Just before he blacked out and you and your two assisting officers arrived on the scene, Mr. Tumorington admitted to me that he knew murder, in and of itself, was *always* morally wrong. Perhaps it was a first genuine step on his path to atonement. Only time will tell."

"I hope you are correct, Esther," agreed Detective Giztips, the eternal optimist, despite his numerous firsthand experiences with humanity's well-documented dark side. "For what it's worth, the team in charge of Hamish's security reports that he has been particularly contrite and docile since his recapture. Let's hope his statement was more than a temporary battlefield conversion."

"Yes," agreed Esther. "Do you have any other questions for me, Detective?"

"Yes, Esther, I suppose I still do have one. While we have both judiciously avoided the proverbial elephant in the room, I must now ask: What if, instead of crazily charging you with the clear and obvious intent to kill, Hamish had simply turned and run away? Would you have still shot him?"

"A fair and straightforward question, Detective," said Esther candidly. "You know me well, my friend. Your query is one that, despite the considerable attention I have since given it, I cannot honestly answer. The good news is that since your question is purely hypothetical, we will never need to know. However, one thing is for certain: You and your backup team were already well on your way to the scene by the time I had no other choice but to shoot and would almost certainly have caught Mr. Tumorington in any event."

"I can live with that answer, Esther," said Detective Giztips. "And I know you can too."

"If you have no further questions, Detective, I would now like to go home and get some much-needed rest."

"Certainly, Esther. Let me conclude this interview by sincerely thanking you once again for your excellent, if admittedly unorthodox, help in bring the Hamish P. Tumorington affair to a most successful conclusion. Thanks to your undaunting courage, tremendous perseverance, and superior sleuthing skills, you and Clive are once again safe and a heinous convicted murderer is in the custody of the police."

"Thank you, Detective Giztips. That is very high praise from a man so accomplished and respected. Our paths, I am certain, will continue to cross."

Montgomery and Ernesta Quaddlelooper spend more time cruising than Barack Hussein Obama does playing golf.

Chapter 32

Aftermath

The sworn statement of Clive Endive Ogive IV, taken later on the very same day that Detective Adam Giztips had interviewed Esther in his office, corroborated everything Esther had said—not that anyone in the know had the slightest bit of doubt that it would. Esther was immediately and completely exonerated of any and all potential wrongdoing. Technically, she could have been charged with breaking and entering for her brief clandestine visit to room ten of Steele's Family Motel & RV Resort, but Detective Giztips knew that not a single prosecutor in the entire country (except, of course, for Eric Holder) would touch that ill-fated can of worms with the proverbial ten-foot pole. To the contrary, within days of her fateful confrontation with Hamish P. Tumorington, Esther stories were dominating the local, national and international news; within a week, she had become something of an American heroine. A Gallup survey, in fact, showed that 98.6% of Americans "strongly agreed" or "agreed" that she had acted properly.

As expected, the left-worshiping sycophants who had surreptitiously infiltrated the mainstream media over the past several decades did their best to discredit and dismiss Esther's meteoric rise to fame, but to no avail. One particularly egotistical and ill-informed talking head on MSNBC had the utter audacity and sheer stupidity to suggest that Esther should have brought a whistle instead of a gun to her potentially deadly confrontation with Hamish P. Tumorington. (At least that was what Esther had been told; with an entire national viewership of less than thirty thousand—of whom only forty-seven had an intelligence quotient in triple digits—it was difficult not to dismiss the ongoing theatrics of that particularly vain self-anointed "celebrity" out of hand.) Such sophomoric drivel only caused Esther's manic popularity with her adoring public to skyrocket to even loftier heights.

Five days following the incident, the Obama administration released its official statement, one that was uncharacteristically muted and terse. "This senseless tragedy is a paradigm example why guns of all kinds should be kept out of the hands of all Americans," pontificated White House Press Secretary Jay Carney, adding somberly, "if the president had a son, he would surely look like Hamish P. Tumorington."

For Esther, the weeks that followed became one gigantic blur. She made extended appearances on the Rush Limbaugh, Mark Levin, Sean Hannity and Glenn Beck radio shows. Rush, breaking with his normal routine of not having guests, spent close to an hour with Esther joyfully eviscerating the idiotic policies and unconstitutional proposals of the Obama administration on everything from gun control to anthropogenic global warming. Subsequent surveys confirmed that, except for the joint appearance of the two Presidents Bush, it was the most listened-to radio talk show episode of all time. Esther's lengthy conversation with Mark "The Great One" Levin centered on several of the especially insightful points he had made in his superbly crafted and undeniably accurate treatise on the inherent superiority of conservatism, *Liberty & Tyranny*. Towards the end of their highly animated and well-informed discussion, Mark told Esther that she knew more about the United States Constitution than everyone in the Obama administration combined. Her feisty appearances on the Sean Hannity and Glenn Beck shows, where both discussions focused on how history has proven over and over again that keeping guns in the hands of individual citizens is essential to a populace maintaining true liberty, received similar kudos from tens of millions of thoughtful patriotic listeners across the country.

As typically happens in such cases, Esther's rapid ascent to stardom dissipated almost as quickly—something that did not bother her in the least. In fact, no one was happier when the soul-sucking paparazzi of this world finally moved on to the latest celebrity du jour. Esther, by nature, was an extremely private person and had grown weary of being recognized and hounded everywhere she went. At the end of the day, the only significant long-term consequence of her heroics was the multi-year agreement she had inked to become an official spokesperson for the National Rifle Association, a group whose core values of more individual freedom and less government meddling meshed particularly well with her own. She was proud to accept the Distinguished Achievement Award that was graciously bestowed upon her at the lavish dinner in her honor.

Esther's fame, unfortunately, caused more than a bit of trouble for Old Bunbury. In the days and weeks immediately following her heroics, the front entrance to the club was besieged by a throng of eerily strange and uncannily annoying people from both the United States and around the world. Most of the Old Bunbury members simply avoided going to their beloved club—an option that, though painful, was deemed preferable over having to inch their way through the motley assemblage of low-information voters clogging the purposefully understated Old Bunbury entrance. For a while, a small ad hoc group calling itself Occupy Old Bunbury marched the streets, not at all sure what its cause was, but nonetheless having a helluva good time chanting hackneyed peace and love slogans, drinking Jose Cuervo straight from the bottle, and merrily puffing away on hand-rolled Mary Jane. (Apparently, they all were on vacation from their day jobs.) The fact that the Board of Directors had to pay a security firm six figures to prevent this bizarre miscellany from the dregs of humanity from sneaking onto the club's hallowed grounds did not exactly help the club's profit and loss statement for the year—not that, at the end of the day, anyone at Old Bunbury really gave a black-footed ferret's foot about that sort of thing. Besides, Jay Morris could always make it up in food and beverage.

The Old Bunbury Board of Directors, while certainly not upset with Esther for singlehandedly rescuing their revered, hostage-taken president and seeing that a heinous convicted murderer was once again returned to jail—to the contrary, her status at the club, if that were possible, rose to even loftier heights with all but a few of the especially ornery and obstinate members—wasn't particularly enamored with the fact that her heroics had once again unwittingly thrust the club into the limelight. To its members, Old Bunbury was, first and foremost, an extremely private and highly cherished sanctuary—a hallowed and sacred home away from home that placed the safety and security of its members above all else. Wise men and women that they were, however, the Old Bunbury Board of Directors knew full well that their club's unwanted exposure and fleeting fame would soon enough pass. And it did.

During her whirlwind few weeks as an international talk-radio phenomenon, Esther imparted more political truth and life wisdom than Barack Hussein Obama has during his entire pathetic presidency.

Chapter 33

Back to Normal—Again

It was a glorious early-November day at Old Bunbury—one of the most desirable and picture-perfect places in the entire world. The dappled sunlight shone brightly through wisps of scattered cirrus clouds; the asters, toad lilies, goldenrod, Russian sage, and Japanese anemone remained in resplendent bloom; the leaves of the towering oaks, maples, and elms continued to glow their glorious cardinal-red and golden hues; the temperature was a perfect 72 degrees Fahrenheit (22.22 degrees Celsius); the humidity remained appreciably lower than was typical for this time of year. All—except for the unfortunate and disturbing fact that Barack Hussein Obama was still president of the United States—was right in the world.

Esther had been sitting in the cramped and cluttered office of Jay Morris—some things in this world just never change—for the past hour, eagerly catching up on all things Old Bunbury with her favorite club manager in the entire world. It was only her third day back at work since her fateful encounter with the nefarious and once-again-incarcerated Hamish P. Tumorington. (Like virtually all of the fallen, Hamish had eventually been gotten the better of by his unchecked hubris; unlike nearly everyone, so had his Old Bunbury-spawned addiction to wordplay.) Esther's celebrity status, to the great relief of all concerned, was continuing on its steady path of appreciable decline.

"So, Jay," Esther said, "I understand that you are finally going to make it to New Zealand."

"It's good to know that despite all that has happened to you these past few months, your encyclopedic knowledge of this great club remains fully intact," Jay said, the touch of sarcasm clearly noticeable in his voice. "Yes, it is indeed true. The wonderful people associated with the Golf Manager's Association of New Zealand have been gracious enough to invite me to be a guest speaker at their upcoming national conference in Auckland. I have been asked to address the particularly thorny and universally challenging issue of successfully dealing with difficult employees. My wife, Eleanor, and I are very much looking forward to our trip."

"Yes, I heard," said Esther. "I know that you both will have a wonderful time. I will, of course, be happy to put together a must-see list of attractions for your visit. And don't worry—you can count on me to keep close tabs on Old Bunbury operations while you are away. We certainly wouldn't want any major issues to arise when you are off gallivanting halfway around the world. By the way, what do *you* know about the subject of difficult employees? You certainly have no experience in that regard," deadpanned Esther.

"I absolutely refuse to take that particular bait," was Jay's only response before he quickly changed the topic. "Esther, I am sure that you already know this, but Rusty Sparnacle, the president of the Kaikoura Whaling & Sailing Club, is visiting Old Bunbury today. He is going to have lunch in the main dining room with President Clive, Mr. Swank, Mr. Bumbery, and Mr. Le Fever." Glancing up at the old-fashioned numbered wall clock on his wall—one that actually still featured a red functioning second hand—Jay added, "I'm guessing that they have already arrived."

"I know, Jay. Why do you think I came to work in the first place?" With that, Esther left Jay's office and marched straight into the dining room, there to find the quintet that included many of her favorite private club members in the entire world.

"Gentlemen!" beamed Esther. "It is so nice to see you. I see that an especially esteemed guest has joined one of Old Bunbury's most infamous fearsome foursomes. Hello,

Mr. Sparnacle," Esther said, looking directly at the man who had so graciously coordinated the gala dinner in her honor at the exclusive and prestigious Kaikoura Whaling & Sailing club. "Welcome back to Old Bunbury."

"I am so very honored to have been invited for lunch and golf at Kaikoura's wonderful sister club, Esther," he said. "You *do* know that you have become something of a world-wide celebrity, young lady. Even our quaint *Marlborough Express* has been faithfully tracking your every movement."

"That's very nice. However, like you and everyone here at Old Bunbury, I am greatly relieved that most of my fleeting fame is now a thing of the past and that things at the club are finally returning to normal."

"Amen to that," echoed Clive for the entire table. "So, Esther, I assume you have purposely chosen to grace Old Bunbury with an appearance on this especially fine day because you are going to wait on our table—that is, of course, unless you have something more pressing on your schedule. Perhaps another talk-radio appearance?"

"It's nice to see that, despite all that you and Old Bunbury have been through of late, you still haven't lost your sense of humor," said Esther.

"As you well know, if you don't have a sense of humor, especially in the wonderful world of private clubs," said Clive, "you might as well hang it up—or admit that you are a closet Democrat."

"If I may ask, Esther, what is Chef Henri's luncheon special?" asked Rusty. "I believe I am going to take a walk on the wild side."

Ignoring the smirks from the other four people at the table—no one at Old Bunbury, except for the rare guest, ever orders the special of the day—Esther said politely, "Today is Wednesday, Mr. Sparnacle, so I am quite confident that Chef Henri has prepared his wonderful oven-roasted free-range chicken breast topped with grilled yellow bell peppers and broccoli florets and served over that short-cut type of macaroni shaped like large grains of rice."

"I'm feeling particularly adventurous, Esther—especially for someone who has reached that particular stage in life where, when I paint the town red, I have to rest for several weeks before applying another coat—so I think I will give it a try," said Rusty.

"I assume the rest of you will have your usual fare," said Esther. It was a statement rather than a question.

"Of course," the four said in meek unison.

"One more thing, Esther," Clive said, "before you place our orders. I want to confirm in person what I am sure you already well know about a recent decision made by the Old Bunbury Board of Directors. After a fair amount of discussion, we unanimously agreed to fund an annual scholarship in your name for a current employee, or an immediate member of his or her family, to attend their choice of Harvard, Yale, Boston College, *The* Ohio State University, or the University of Florida. Congratulations! We think it is an especially fitting way of honoring all that you have done for Old Bunbury these past many decades as well as preserving in perpetuity the legacy of our club's most famous—or should I say infamous—waitress."

"Yes, I did hear about that. What a wonderful honor! Thank you, boss. Please extend my sincere gratitude to everyone on the board. When I first found out about the decision, I must admit that, at least for a moment or two, I was concerned about the recipient being accepted at the school of his or her choice. This may come as a shock, but we have more than a few people working here who don't always have both oars in the water. But silly me! I know that the collective Old Bunbury membership has more than enough clout to make sure that whoever receives the scholarship will be able to attend the college that he or she prefers."

"Thank you for your confidence in us," deadpanned Clive. With that, Esther headed for the kitchen, presumably to turn in the orders.

Not long after, Esther dutifully returned, deferentially trailed by the tray-toting newest member of the Old Bunbury staff, busboy Kilgore Trout III. (Kilgore, as it happened, was the great-grandson of the long-deceased Leo Trout, now internationally known and revered for his pioneering work on behalf of Bermuda's Royal Ornithological Society.) When Esther had placed the last of the five plates, Clive, glancing around the table, remarked sarcastically, "Thank you, Esther. I know it is rather amazing, but I believe that everyone has gotten the correct order."

"Orzo it seems," deadpanned Danny Bumbery, looking directly at Rusty Sparnacle's lunch.

"That is just god-awful," groaned Rusty. "However, as you three well know, we Kiwis also know a thing or two about the joy of wordplay. So as long as our conversation is headed in that dubious direction, let me ask you all this: 'What is another way of saying that an octet of sheep consumed plants in the family polemoniaceae?'"

"Not a clue," Clive said for the silenced group. "What?"

"Eight flocks ate phlox."

Even Esther grimaced upon hearing the uncharted depths to which the jovial quintet's pun-making had now sunk. "I believe that Mr. Sparnacle and Mr. Bumbery's observations serve as the perfect segue for one final question I have before I take my leave from the table," she said.

"Certainly, Esther," agreed Clive amicably. Nothing Esther could do or say was going to spoil such a perfect day. (Well, almost nothing.)

"What do you call repeated denials from a Scottish nutritionist living in Rochester, Minnesota?"

"I don't know, Esther," answered a befuddled Clive. "Universal health care at its finest?"

"Obamacare in action?" offered J. Eaton Swank hopefully.

"Crass negativity from one of the seventeen illegal aliens in this country who actually has earned a legitimate college degree?" chimed in a hopeful Dr. Art Le Fever.

"All good answers," chuckled Esther, "but there is a better one."

"What's that, Esther?"

"Mayo nays, gentlemen; mayonnaise."

The entrance to Old Bunbury circa 2040.

Acknowledgments

Several wonderfully generous people were helpful in making my latest major literary effort a reality. You all know who you are, so there is no need for me to gush. Special kudos go to Mike Szabo of Big Mike Design (www.BigMikeDesign.com) for his magic with a few of this book's photographs as well as to the entire team at Dog Ear Publishing Company (www.DogEarPublishing.net). Of course, Cody Pollock Spitzig, my beautiful wife of nearly thirty-two years, once again topped my support group. Thank you, Cody, for your excellent plot suggestions, patient and meticulous proofreading, and, far more importantly, unwavering love and reluctant acceptance of my one or two foibles.

I have often been asked whether Clive, Esther, and the Old Bunbury Golf Links & Reading Club are real or fictional. The best way to answer this question, I believe, is by citing one of my favorite snippets from J. K. Rowling's seventh and last book in her wildly successful and immensely entertaining Harry Potter series, *Harry Potter and the Deathly Hallows*. When Harry, near the end of the novel, asks Dumbledore, "Is this real? Or has this been happening inside my head?" the ever-astute Dumbledore sagely answers, "Of course it's happening inside your head, Harry, but why on earth should that mean that it is not real?"

An early reader of this manuscript suggested that I consider "toning down" the political commentary a bit—and, to a point, I did. What remain are Clive and Esther's inarguably potent refutations of some of the more malicious distortions that regularly emanate from the Obama White House. It is also my own personally satisfying way of irritating and poking fun at the uppity, self-righteous far left—humorless people who never let logic, facts or the desires of the majority get in the way of their perverse pursuit of America's demise.

I must say, I have thoroughly enjoyed my career in the private club world, the majority of it as a general manager and, for the past dozen years, as an entrepreneur specializing in executive search and operations and governance consulting. What I don't miss are those periodic and impassioned diatribes from disgruntled but misinformed members ("Our dues are the highest in the northern hemisphere." or "We've paying our staff at least double the going rate." or "The entire kitchen staff are nothing but a bunch of unabashed thieves." or "If we only had fifty more Social Members, all the club's many problems would be solved."). I am now at that stage of life when I don't have to put up with such utter nonsense, and I extend my sincere condolences to those—both members and management—who still must.

I always like to hear from my loyal readers, so please feel free to get in touch with me at your convenience; the best way to reach me is to e-mail me at normspitzig@ hotmail.com. I also encourage you to follow @ClivetheClubGuy on Twitter to keep up with my latest "Twisdoms" (Twitter wisdom), political gibes, private club and golf commentary, and ongoing attempts at sarcastic humor. While my passion for personal freedom, individual responsibility, and the unadulterated truth continues to appreciate, my tolerance for incompetent and close-minded people, indifferent and mediocre performance, and excessive and obtrusive bureaucracy remains in steady decline. I, like far more people than the left will openly acknowledge, remain steadfastly true to the Founding Fathers' Great American Dream.

In the past five years, I like to think that I have penned the definitive universal operational and governance handbook for the wonderful world of private clubs, a page-turning murder mystery set in one of the world's most exclusive and distinguished private clubs, and a riveting autobiography complete with a baker's dozen of timeless core life lessons—and now this Clive and Esther reprise adventure. I sincerely hope you had as much fun reading this latest offering as I did writing it.

No one, absolutely no one, knows more about the wonderful world of private clubs than Clive Endive Ogive IV.

About the Author

Norm Spitzig is internationally recognized as a successful entrepreneur; a leading business consultant; an eloquent, visionary, humorous, and engaging speaker on a variety of important business and lifestyle topics; and an all-around good egg. His groundbreaking book *Perspectives on Club Management*—now more than thirty years old—continues to inspire and challenge private club owners, directors, managers, and students around the world. Norm, qua Clive Endive Ogive IV, is also the more recent author of three *very* funny and insightful books, *Private Clubs in America and around the World* and *Murder and Mayhem at Old Bunbury*, both of which are available at www.CliveEndiveOgiveIV. com, Amazon, many private club golf pro shops, and fine bookstores everywhere. The third, *How Now, Norm's Tao,* is Norm's autobiography, a book that has been recently hailed as a "powerful and poignant memoir by one of the most accomplished and unique writers to grace contemporary American literature." *How Now, Norm's Tao*, together with *Soul on Nice*, is available at www.NormSpitzig.com and from Amazon and assorted bookstores.

Norm's leadership and professional contributions to the worldwide private club industry have been varied and significant. Elected a national director of the Club Managers Association of America (CMAA) in 1989, he served as its national president in 1995—the same year he became one of the original six general managers to earn the prestigious lifetime Master Club Manager (MCM) designation.

Norm currently serves as a principal & senior partner in Master Club Advisors (www.MasterClubAdvisors.com), publisher of the premier newsletter for leaders in the worldwide private club industry, *Club Management Perspectives*, and now regarded by more and more leaders in the global private club industry as *the* "general manager executive search firm of choice." Norm's Board of Directors' leadership orientations, strategic planning sessions, and inspirational talks have been very well received at national, regional, and local meetings of many professional associations, company retreats, and great individual private clubs on six continents. He has the singular honor of having been twice named the club industry's educator of the year.

Norm, who doggedly continues his improbable, and admittedly weird, pursuit of logging one hundred thousand running miles before he ascends to the great private club in the sky, resides in the historic town of Mount Dora, Florida, with his beautiful bride, Cody, and ball-obsessed chocolate Labrador, Lucy.

The author—his rakish grin and dapper demeanor on full display.

CPSIA information can be obtained
at www.ICGtesting.com
Printed in the USA
BVOW03s0203050917
493949BV00001B/5/P

9 781457 521706